5-MINUTE MARVEL STORIES

MARVEL

New York

"Keep Away From Kraven the Hunter" written by Kevin Shinick, based upon the Marvel comic book series *Spider-Man*.
Illustrated by Craig Rousseau and Hi-Fi Design

"The X-Men's First Mission" adapted by Alison Lowenstein, based upon the Marvel comic book series *The X-Men*.
Illustrated by the Disney Storybook Art Group

"A Brother's Battle" adapted by Clarissa Wong, based upon the Marvel comic book series *The Avengers*.
Illustrated by Pat Olliffe and Hi-Fi Design

"Iron Man's New Armor" written by Alison Lowenstein, based upon the Marvel comic book series *Iron Man*.
Illustrated by Craig Rousseau and Hi-Fi Design

"Spider-Man vs. Sandman" written by Alison Lowenstein, based upon the Marvel comic book series *Spider-Man*.
Illustrated by Craig Rousseau and Hi-Fi Design

"Surprise Attack" written by Clarissa Wong, based upon the Marvel comic book series *Iron Man*.
Illustrated by Craig Rousseau and Hi-Fi Design

"Captain America Returns" adapted by Alison Lowenstein, based upon the Marvel comic book series *The Avengers*.
Illustrated by Pat Olliffe and Hi-Fi Design

"Spider-Man vs. the Sinister Six" adapted by Tomas Palacois, based upon the Marvel comic book series *Spider-Man*.
Illustrated by Todd Nauck and Hi-Fi Design

"Hawkeye and the Mighty Avengers" written by Nachie Castro, based upon the Marvel comic book series *The Avengers*.
Illustrated by Mike Norton and Hi-Fi Design

"Desert Brawl" written by Clarissa Wong, based upon the Marvel comic book series *The Hulk*.
Illustrated by Val Semeiks and Hi-Fi Design

"Peter Parker's Pictures" written by Alison Lowenstein, based upon the Marvel comic book series *Spider-Man*.
Illustrated by Todd Nauck and Hi-Fi Design

"The Lethal Lair of Red Skull" written by Elizabeth Schaefer, based upon the Marvel comic book series *Captain America*.
Illustrated by Val Semeiks, the Disney Storybook Art Group, and Hi-Fi Design

Printed in the United States of America

First Edition

11 10 9 8 7

FAC-038091-15212

ISBN 978-1-4231-6722-8

marvelkids.com

SUSTAINABLE FORESTRY INITIATIVE Certified Sourcing
www.sfiprogram.org
SFI-00993
This Label Applies To Text Stock Only

TM & © 2012 Marvel & Subs.

TABLE OF CONTENTS

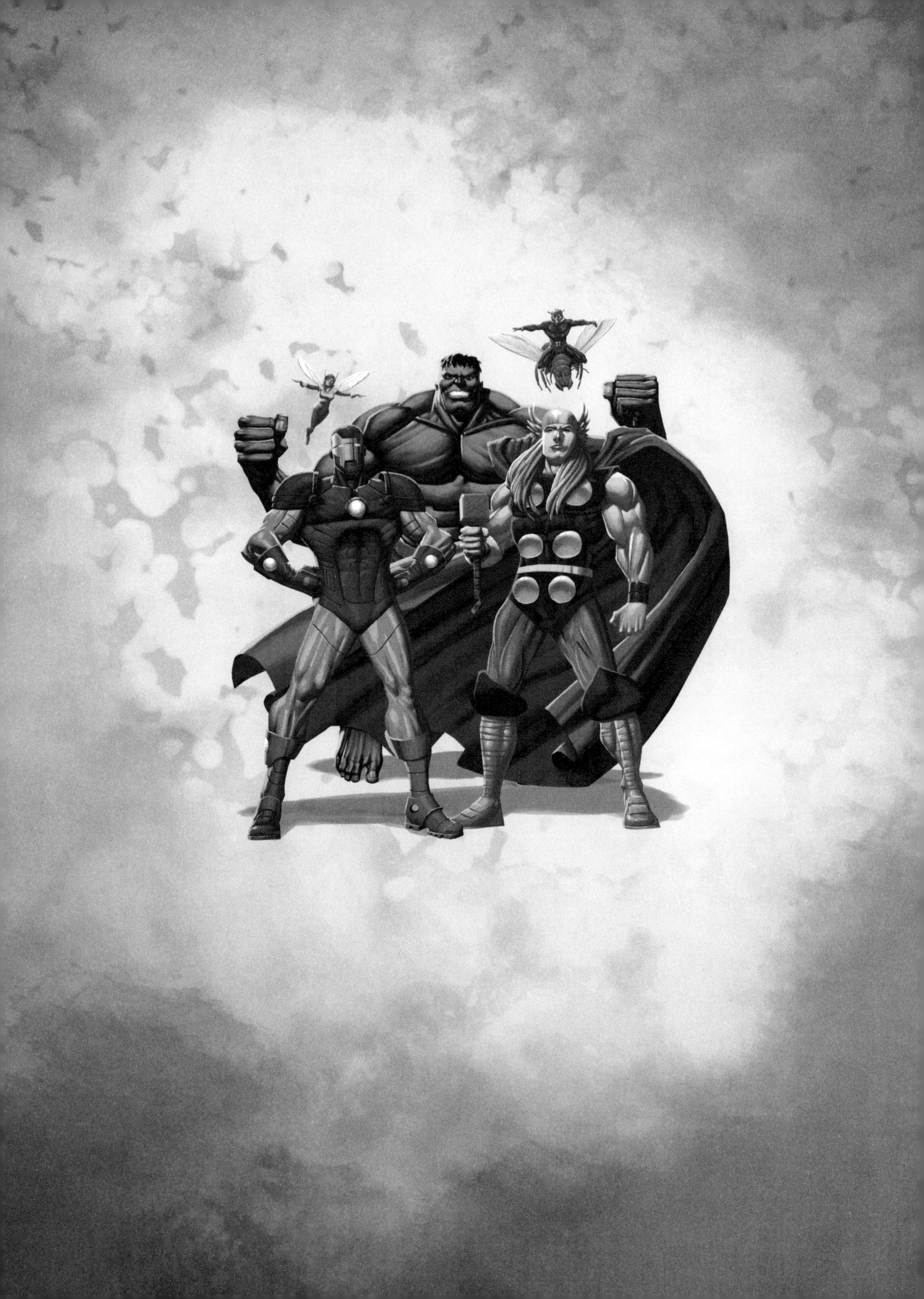

Keep Away From Kraven the Hunter

It was a beautiful Saturday morning in New York City. As the sun rose, so did the Amazing Spider-Man, who was up early and on the hunt for crime. He had already stopped two robberies and webbed up one car thief—all before 7 a.m.!

But now it was time for Spidey to take off his mask and make his way over to the Central Park Zoo. It was time for Peter Parker to have some fun!

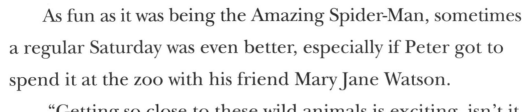

As fun as it was being the Amazing Spider-Man, sometimes a regular Saturday was even better, especially if Peter got to spend it at the zoo with his friend Mary Jane Watson.

"Getting so close to these wild animals is exciting, isn't it, Petey?" Mary Jane asked.

But Peter took a step back. "This might be a little too close," he whimpered. Peter liked pretending to be afraid of things he wasn't in order to protect his secret identity. But suddenly something happened that really did make him worry.

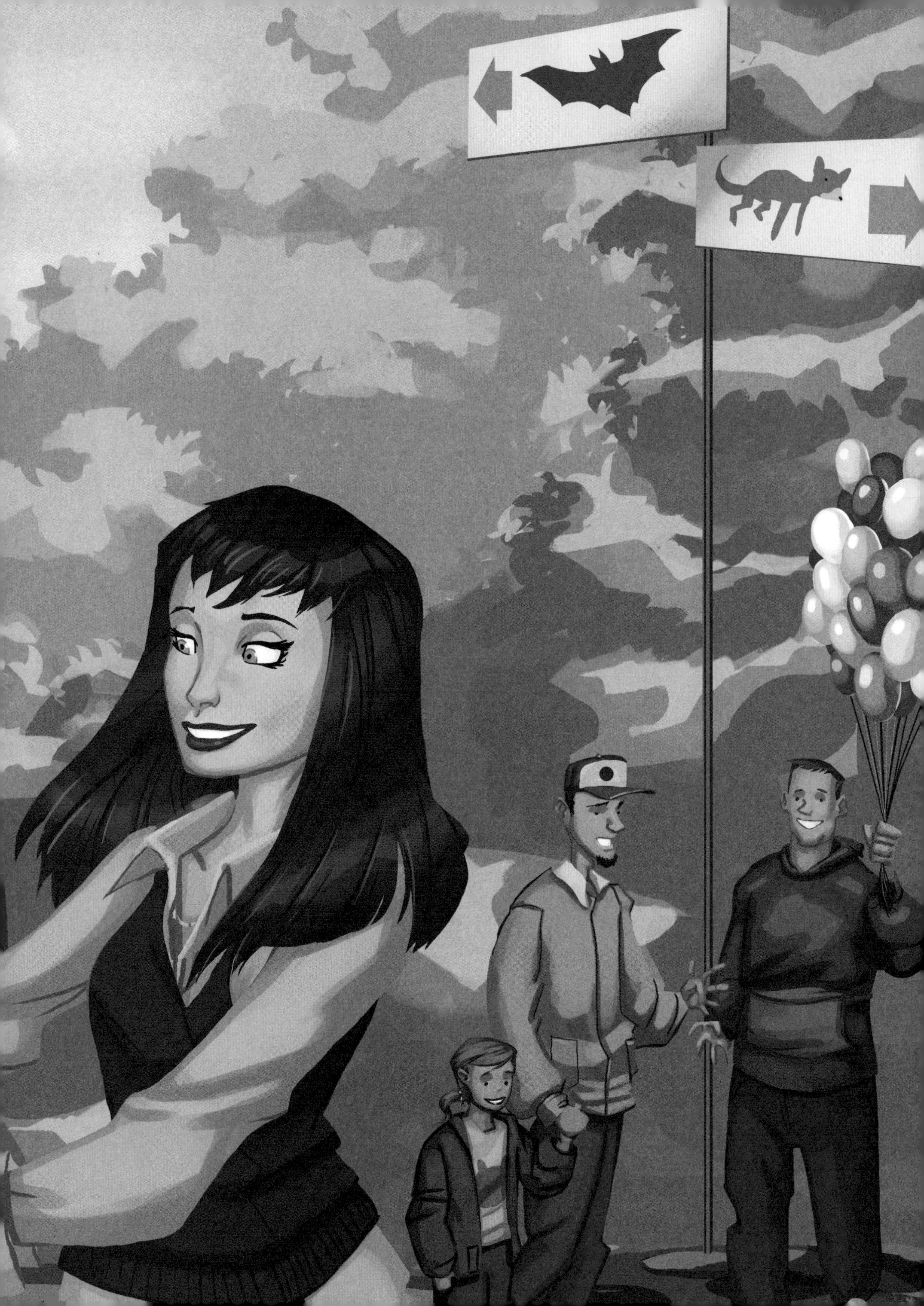

My spider-sense is tingling, thought Peter.
Looks like Spider-Man won't have the afternoon off
after all. Peter wished he could spend more time
enjoying the zoo, but he knew that with great power
came great responsibility.

"Somebody help!" screamed the zoo's janitor. "A gorilla's gotten loose!" And what a giant gorilla it was. He was three times the size of a man with enough power to crush a nearby hot-dog cart. Peter realized that even though the animal was probably just confused, he could still accidentally hurt someone.

With everyone looking at the beast, Peter snuck away
to change into his costume. He hoped Mary Jane wouldn't
notice him leaving, but he was certain that if the gorilla wasn't
enough of a distraction already, surely she'd be distracted by
the sight of her friendly neighborhood Spider-Man.

But when Spider-Man returned, he found somebody
else already on the scene. It was Kraven the Hunter, the
greatest hunter alive. Within a matter of seconds, he
showed the powerful primate who the king of the jungle
really was.

The crowd applauded as Kraven quickly subdued the
gorilla with a choke hold and dragged him back into his
cage. Emerging from the lair, Kraven locked the door
behind him as flashbulbs popped and reporters took
pictures of this newly crowned hero.

Like a leopard returning from a kill, Kraven stood triumphant. His clothes were dirty, and he smelled like the jungle. A reporter shouted, "What are you doing in America, Kraven?"

With the growl of a wildcat, the hunter responded, "I have defeated every animal there is, so today I hunt the most dangerous creature alive . . . man. But not just any man—Spider-Man!"

Spidey couldn't believe his ears. Hunt me? he said to himself. "There must be a mistake," Spidey began. "You didn't come all this way just to squash a spider, did you? Surely you must have me confused with some other charming, handsome, and radioactive web-head." Kraven wasn't amused.

Without warning, Kraven lunged at Spider-Man with the force of a rhino. Luckily the wall-crawler jumped out of the way just in time.

"Whoa! You must be lost, pal. The auditions for *The Lion King* are downtown," Spidey cracked. But even as he joked, Spider-Man could feel how strong Kraven was. He had the strength of an elephant and the speed of a panther. Unfortunately, he also had something else.

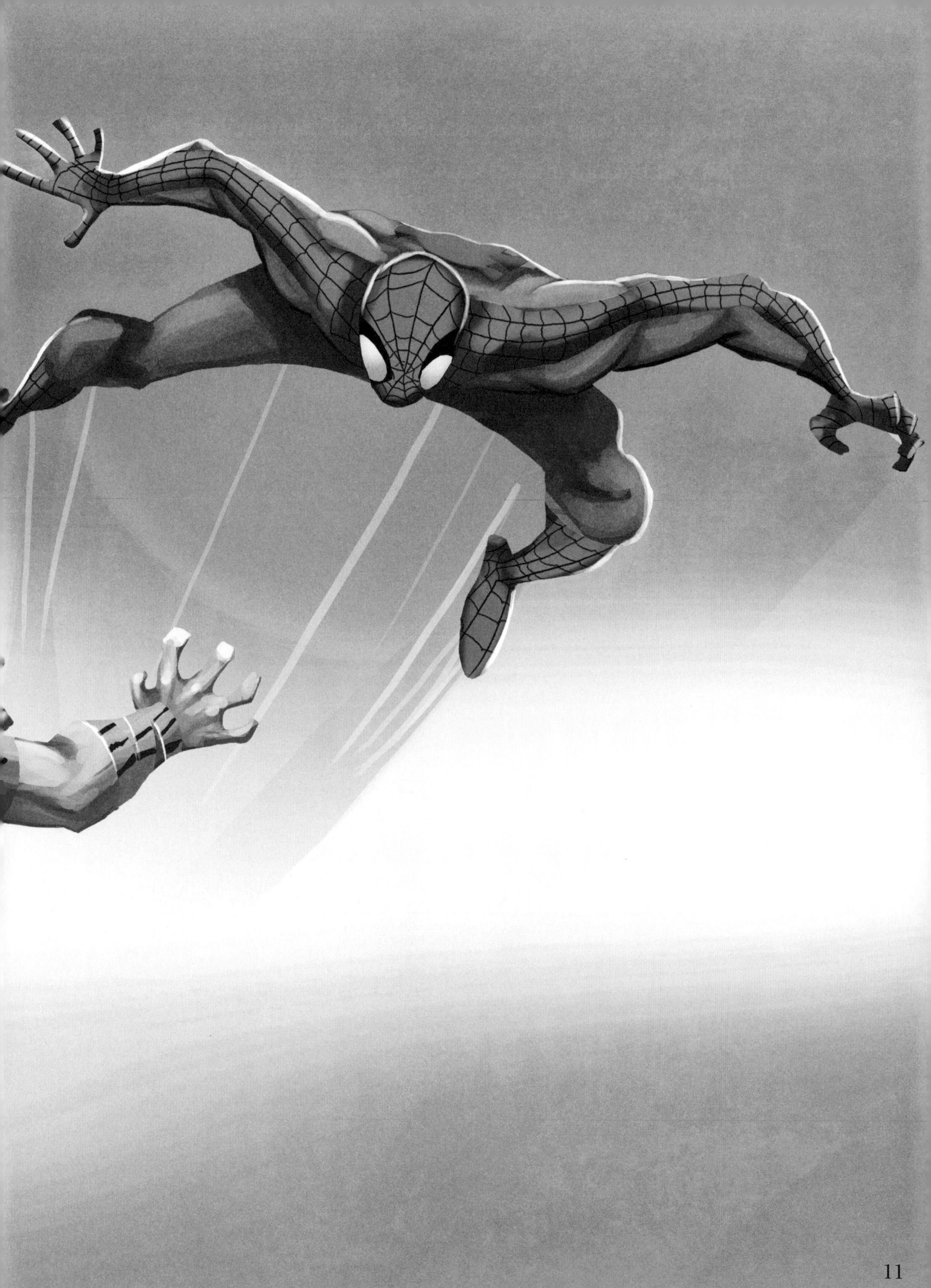

Spider-Man is tougher than I imagined, Kraven said to himself. I will have to cheat by sticking him with this poisonous venom I took from a snake. "You can't win, Spider-Man," roared the hunter. "I have the secrets of the jungle on my side!"

But before Kraven could inject Spider-Man
with the poisonous venom, the web-slinger swung
into action. "That's fine with me." Spidey laughed.
"All I need are the secrets of a spider!"

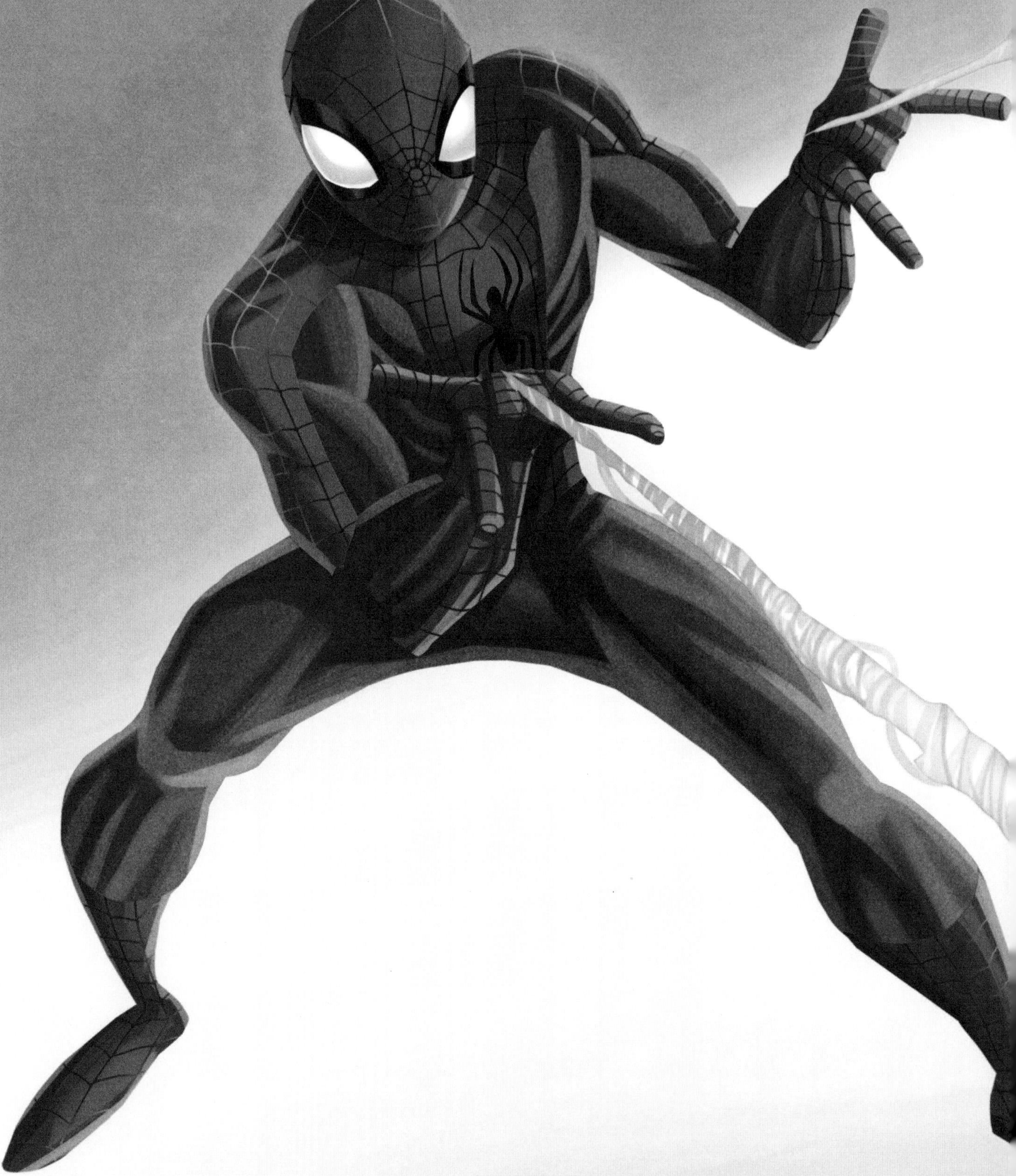

Spider-Man did it! He captured the greatest hunter alive. Without missing a beat, Spidey fired his web-shooters so that Kraven wouldn't be able to hunt or hurt anyone else.

When he was finished, Spidey walked over to Kraven and apologized. "Sorry I had to ruin your birthday," Spidey said.

"My birthday?" cried Kraven. "Why would you think it's my birthday?"

"Well," said Spidey, "you look like a monkey. And you smell like one, too."

With that, Spider-Man turned to leave. He had to change out of his costume and get back to Mary Jane. But even with the unexpected arrival of a Super Villain on a Saturday afternoon, it was still a great day for both Peter Parker and the Amazing Spider-Man.

THE UNCANNY X-MEN

The X-Men's First Mission

Professor Charles Xavier showed the Uncanny X-Men his new invention, a machine called Cerebro. This device was able to locate other mutants with special powers, such as the X-Men. The X-Men used their mutant abilities to help people, but one mutant, Magneto, was using his powers for evil.

Professor X knew Magneto, and he told the X-Men their story.

"His name was once Erik Magnus, and he used to be a good friend of mine. He was one of the first mutants I ever met," Professor X explained. He and Magnus once defeated an evil human named Baron von Strucker, who wanted to use his wealth to conquer and destroy. After meeting the baron, Magnus felt this proved humans were inherently bad. Magnus took all the Baron's gold and waged war on the human race. Now he was attacking an army base.

The X-Men were ready for their first mission as a team and were excited to use their powers for good. They knew they had to stop Magneto and protect the innocent.

Professor X sent them off and wished them luck.

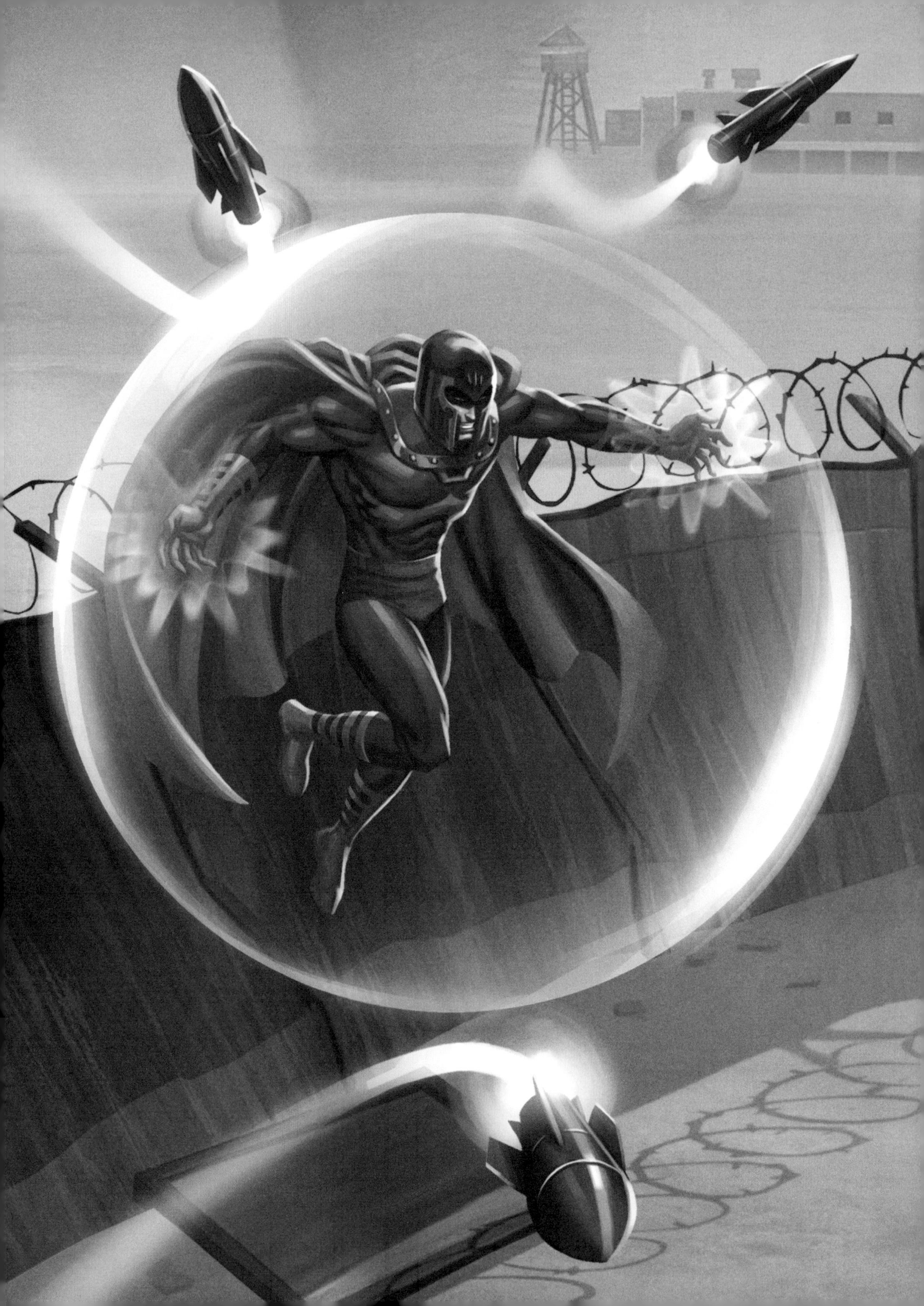

Miles away, Magneto was wreaking havoc across the army base by using his powers to twist metal and control magnetic fields. The army tried to fight back with tanks and missiles, but they were useless against the evil mutant. Soldiers were hiding and running for cover, and that's when Magneto addressed the troops.

"I am Magneto," he began, "and I claim this base in the name of mutantkind."

Just then, the X-Men arrived!

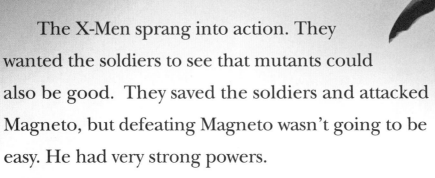

The X-Men sprang into action. They wanted the soldiers to see that mutants could also be good. They saved the soldiers and attacked Magneto, but defeating Magneto wasn't going to be easy. He had very strong powers.

When Cyclops shot an optic blast at Magneto, nothing happened. Cyclops opened his ruby-quartz visor even wider and used the full power of his blast, but Magneto sent metal objects to block Cyclops's attack.

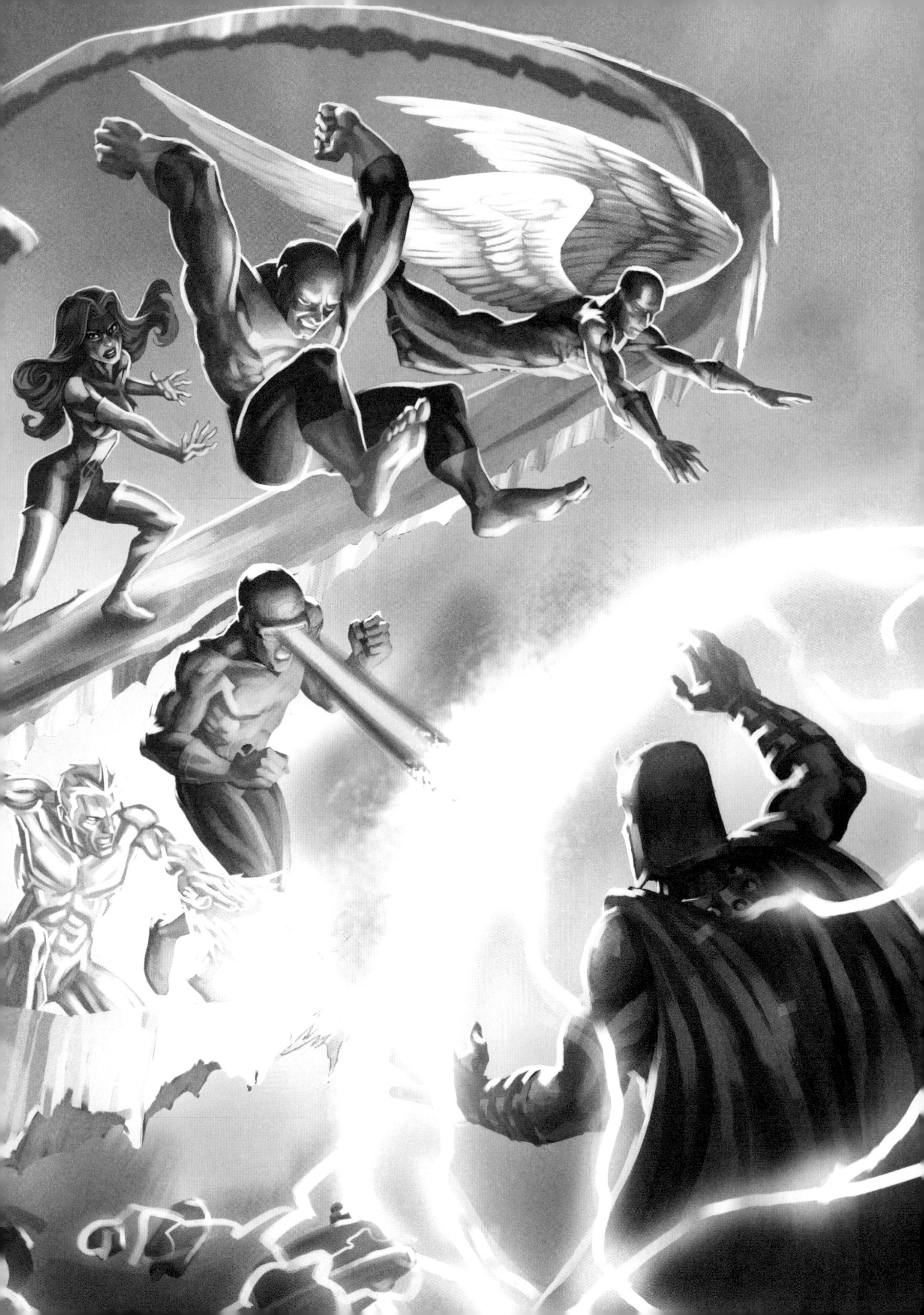

As Cyclops blasted away at the debris, Marvel Girl
used her powers to direct missiles toward Magneto, but his
magnetic powers were able to send them right back at her.

One missile flew toward Angel, who dodged it just in the nick of time. But then Magneto took control of the missile and aimed it back toward Angel. The winged mutant was fast, but the missile was faster.

Several more missiles flew toward Beast, who tried to catch them with his feet—but there were too many to grab, despite Beast's strength. The X-Men were losing.

But then the X-Men got an idea! Magneto was stronger than the individual X-Men, but if they worked together, the X-Men had the power to stop the evil mutant. The X-Men combined their powers and attacked. Quickly realizing he was outnumbered, Magneto sent everything he could directly at the X-Men. The heroes tried to fight back, but it was hard to avoid the flying debris.

The X-Men didn't give up hope. When Magneto attacked again, Marvel Girl covered her teammates with a force field. Magento's attacks were useless now.

So instead, Magneto decided to escape.

When they returned to Professor X, the X-Men told him how disappointed they were about letting Magneto get away.

"On the contrary," the professor said. "I'm very proud of you for stopping the attack and for saving the soldiers," Professor X continued. "Magneto wasn't strong enough to fight you all at once. You did what you set out to do. You stopped the attack and saved innocent people. All of you have done an excellent job."

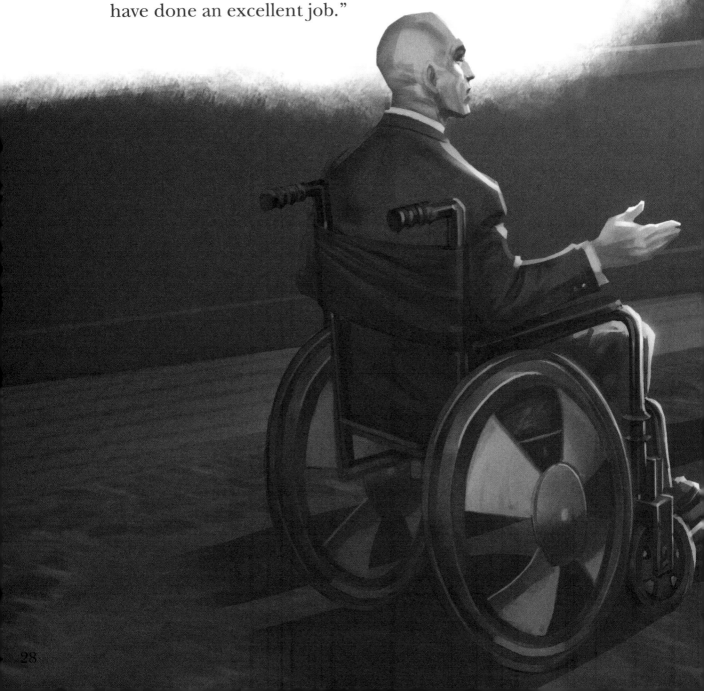

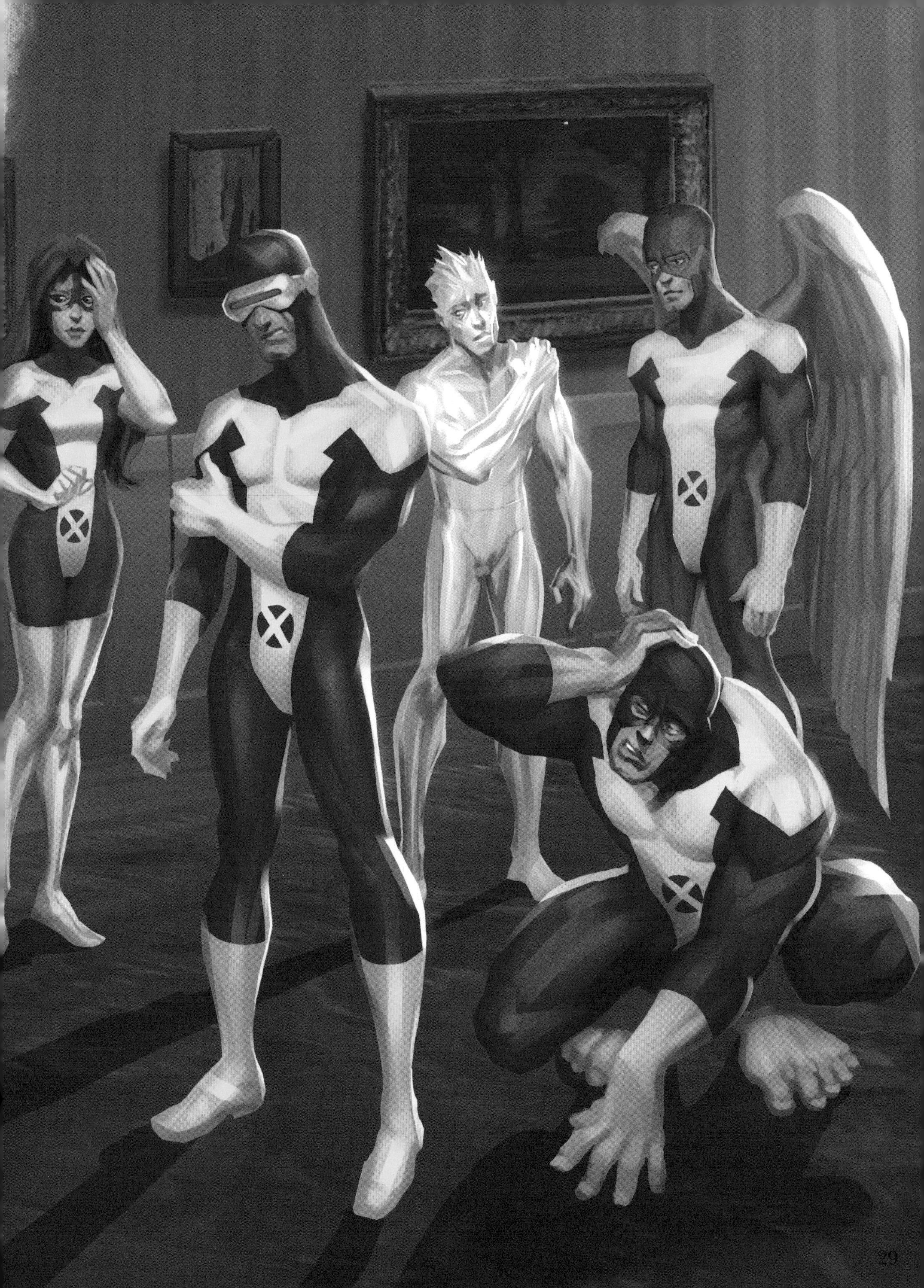

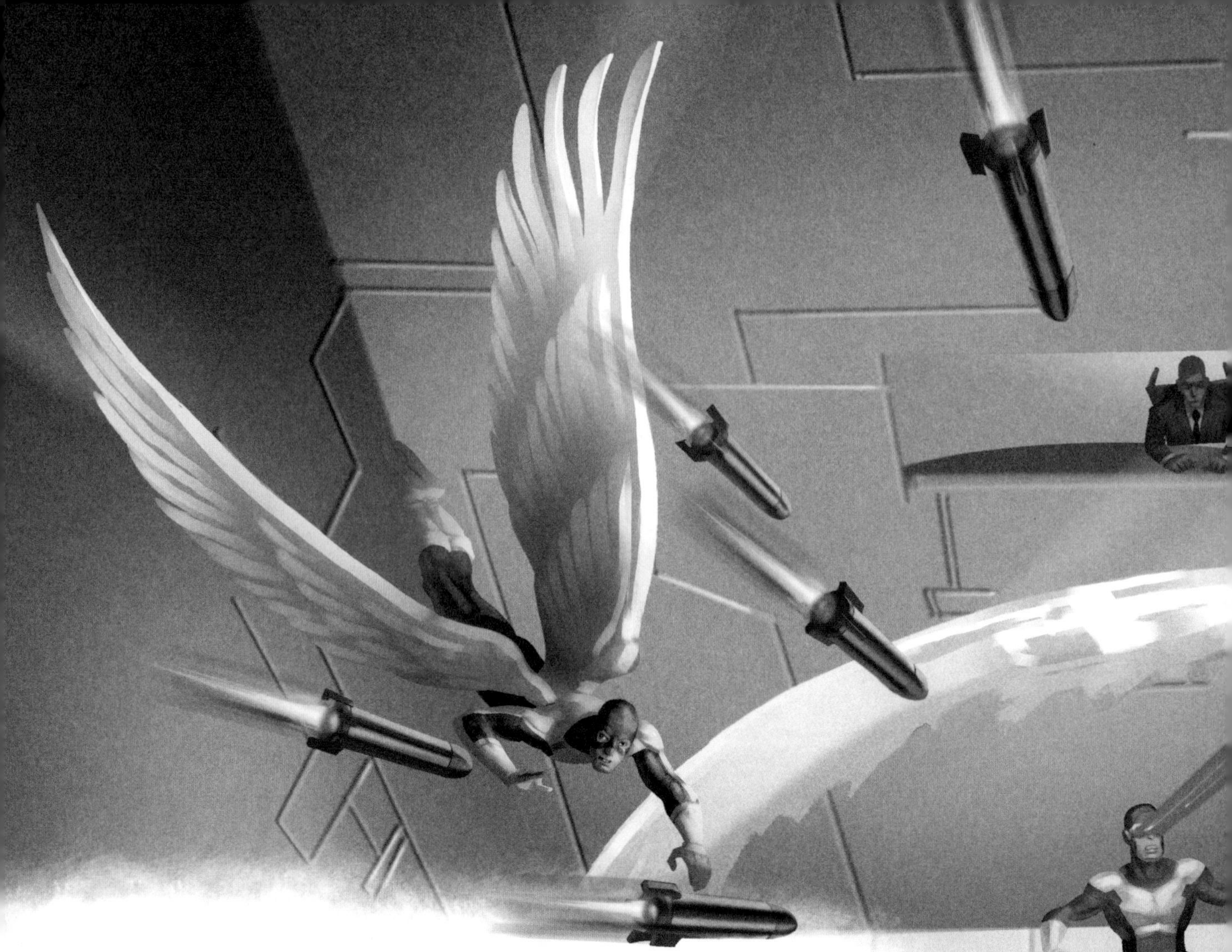

The X-Men knew that this was just their first mission and that they had to train to become better Super Heroes. Over the next few months, they trained in a special gym called the Danger Room. The room was filled with various obstacles that would help the X-Men perfect their abilities.

Missiles and lasers attacked them, trying to duplicate the many challenges they would encounter when battling against evil mutants and other villians.

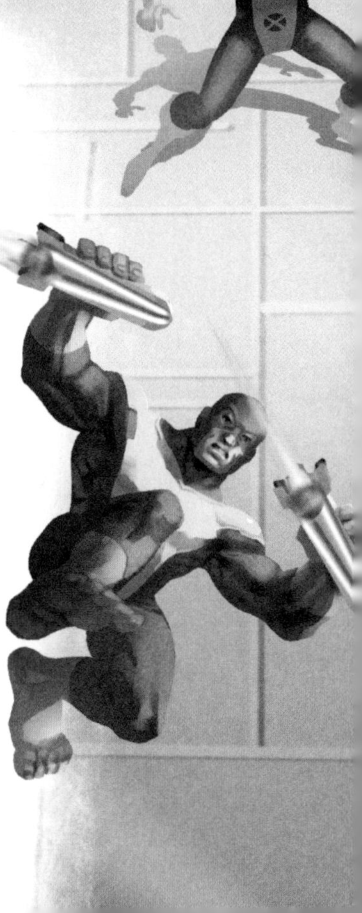

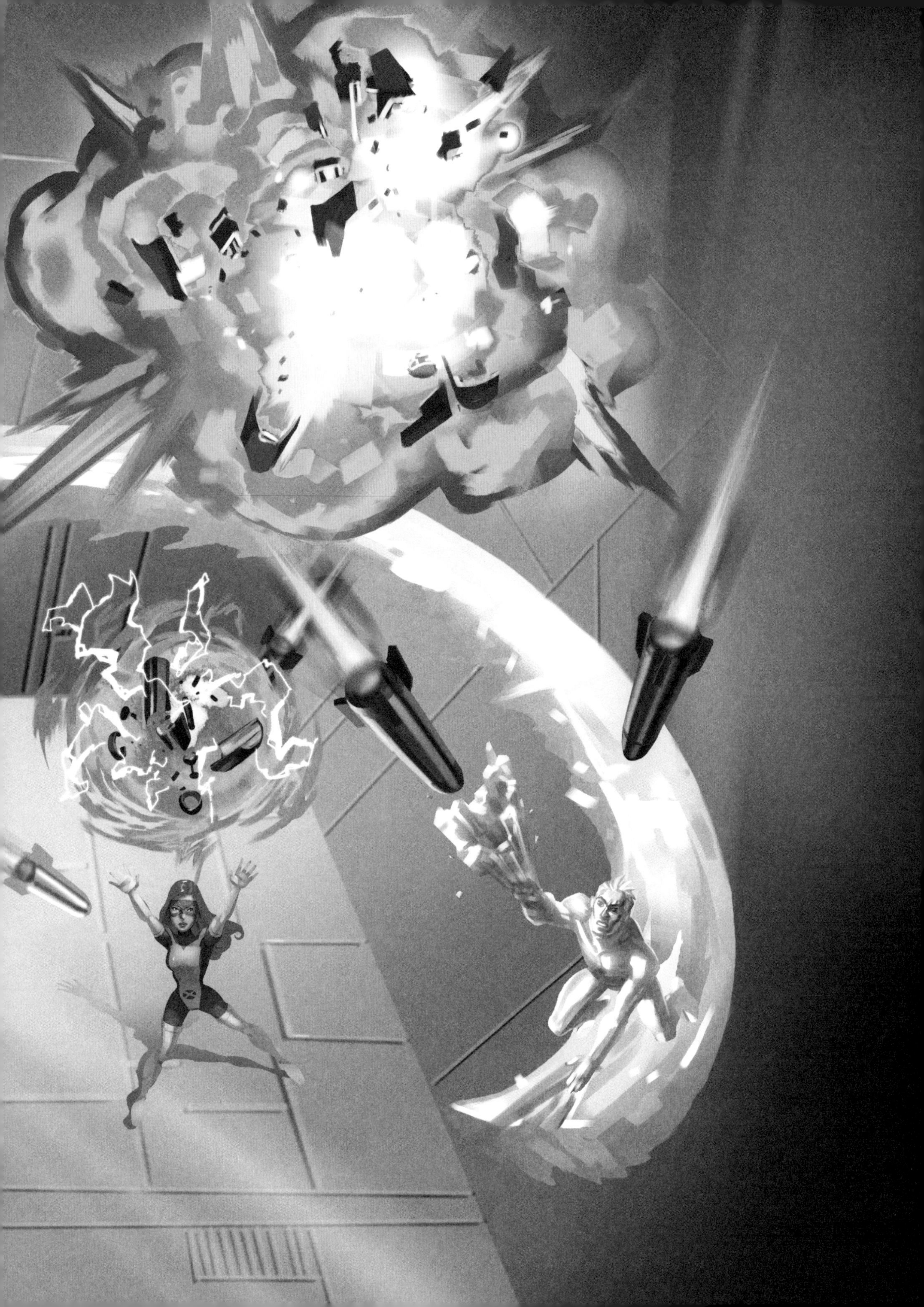

And while his students trained, Professor Xavier used Cerebro to keep a constant watch for good mutants who could join their team—and evil mutants that would need to be defeated. He also kept a close eye on his onetime friend and now enemy, Magneto. Professor X knew the team would have to fight him again, and when they did, the Uncanny X-Men would be ready!

THE MIGHTY THOR

A Brother's Battle

When they were younger, Thor and Loki, the two princes of Asgard, were inseparable. But as they grew older, the brothers grew apart. And when Loki heard Thor was next in line for the throne of Asgard, he knew he should be happy for his brother. But all Loki could feel was incredible jealousy.

Loki disliked how Thor hogged the spotlight by showing off his powers and strength. I have amazing powers, too, Loki thought.

Loki was an expert at magic and playing tricks on the mind, something Thor found irritating as they grew older. Suddenly, Loki felt a horrible urge to crush Thor. He gasped at the thought of this. He did not want to hurt his brother. Yet he had a stronger desire to be king.

Loki planned to trap Thor on the Isle of Silence where no one would find him. Loki would lure his brother there by tricking Thor into rescuing him. With his brother gone, Loki would be the next in line for the throne. Loki was pleased with his selfish plot.

Meanwhile, Thor was on Earth as Dr. Don Blake. Even though he was galaxies away, he was still connected to Asgard—so connected that he could hear Loki's cry for help! Loki was stranded on the Isle of Silence!

Donald Blake immediately transformed into the Mighty Thor to save his brother! Little did he know he was falling right into Loki's trap.

Thor rushed over the Rainbow Bridge to the Isle of
Silence. When he arrived, he did not see his brother.
Worried about Loki, Thor didn't notice the Silent Ones,
trolls who lived belowground on the isle, emerging
from the soil.

Suddenly, the ground shook! Thor tried to gain his
balance as the surface broke into millions of pieces as the
trolls grabbed at him. Then Loki appeared!

"Brother, so glad you made it." Loki cackled. Thor realized it was a trick!

All the trolls attacked Thor at once! They were huge—at least twice the size of Thor! They pulled him underground, trying to take him captive, as Loki had promised they could. Struggling, Thor wrestled with the trolls.

Loki watched Thor's doom with a satisfied smirk. Excited, he raced back to Asgard to claim his spot as the heir to the throne.

Thor had fought many creatures, monsters, and beasts before. But these trolls were big and strong, just like him. His only chance to beat them was with Mjolnir. As he struck his mighty hammer against the ground, bolts of lightning shot out from every direction. As the lightning hit the Silent Ones, the trolls screeched in pain and instantly buried themselves underground.

Once the Silent Ones were defeated, Thor noticed Loki was already gone. Flying above the Bifrost, Thor searched for the Trickster.

Minutes later, he spotted Loki. Effortlessly, Thor plucked him from the Bifrost and flew back to the Isle of Silence. This time, the Silent Ones did not come out. They knew better than to bother Thor; they would be satisfied with Loki as their prisoner.

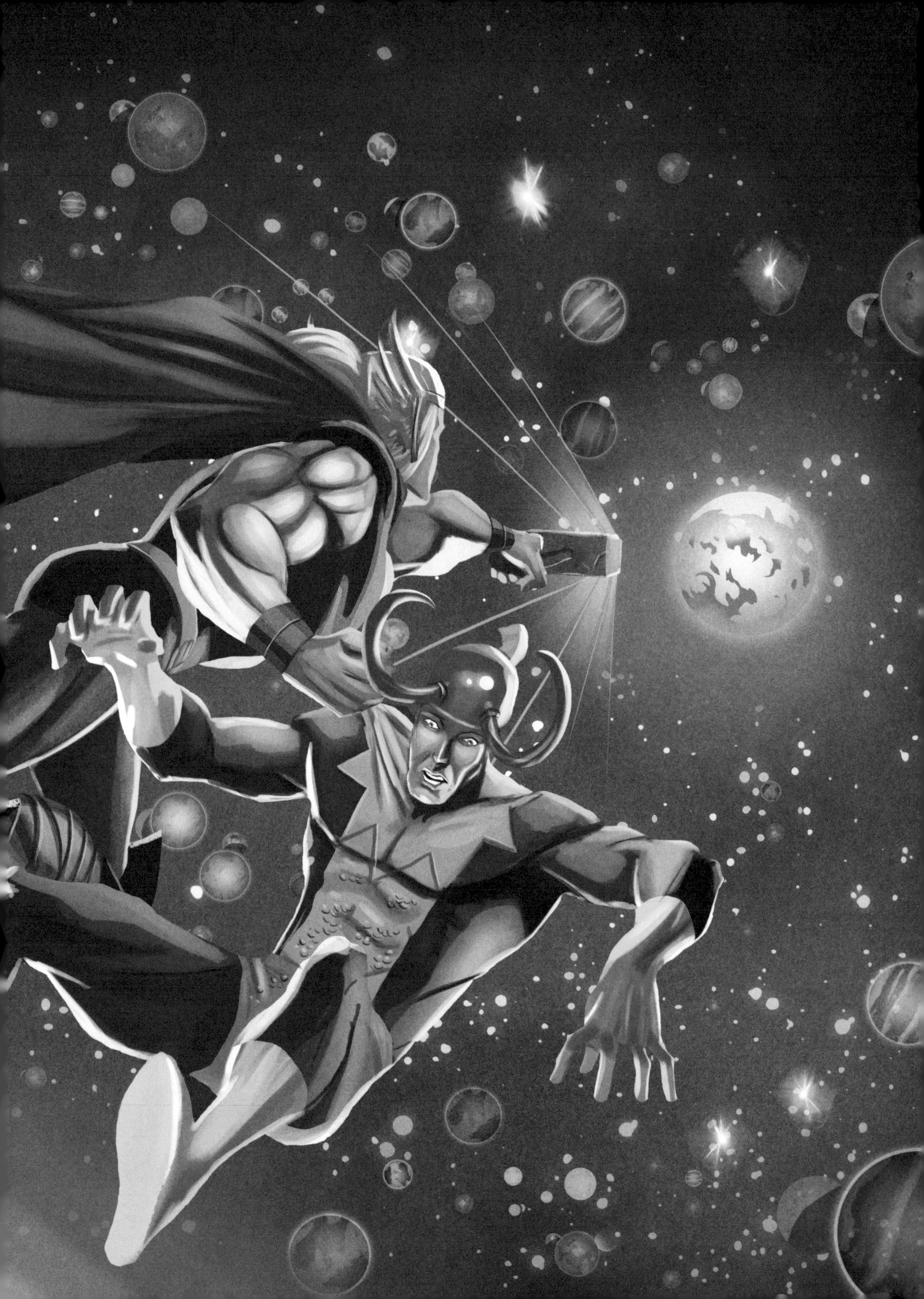

"Why did you bring me back here?" Loki asked, confused. Thor held Loki's collar tight. He did not trust Loki.

"I risked my life to save you . . . only for you to betray me. Why would you do this?" Thor asked. Loki only flashed a mischievous grin. Thor could not imagine what else this trickster was up to.

"You are a prisoner here, Loki. You can return to Asgard when you're ready to be my brother again," Thor said. But Loki was already back to his old ways!

Loki used his magic to make it seem like there were dozens of him! Thor had had enough of his brother's games. With a mighty swing of Mjolnir, Thor knocked out all the illusions until only one was left—the real Loki, who was surprised by Thor's outburst.

"Tell me why you did this, Loki," Thor demanded. But Loki gave no response.

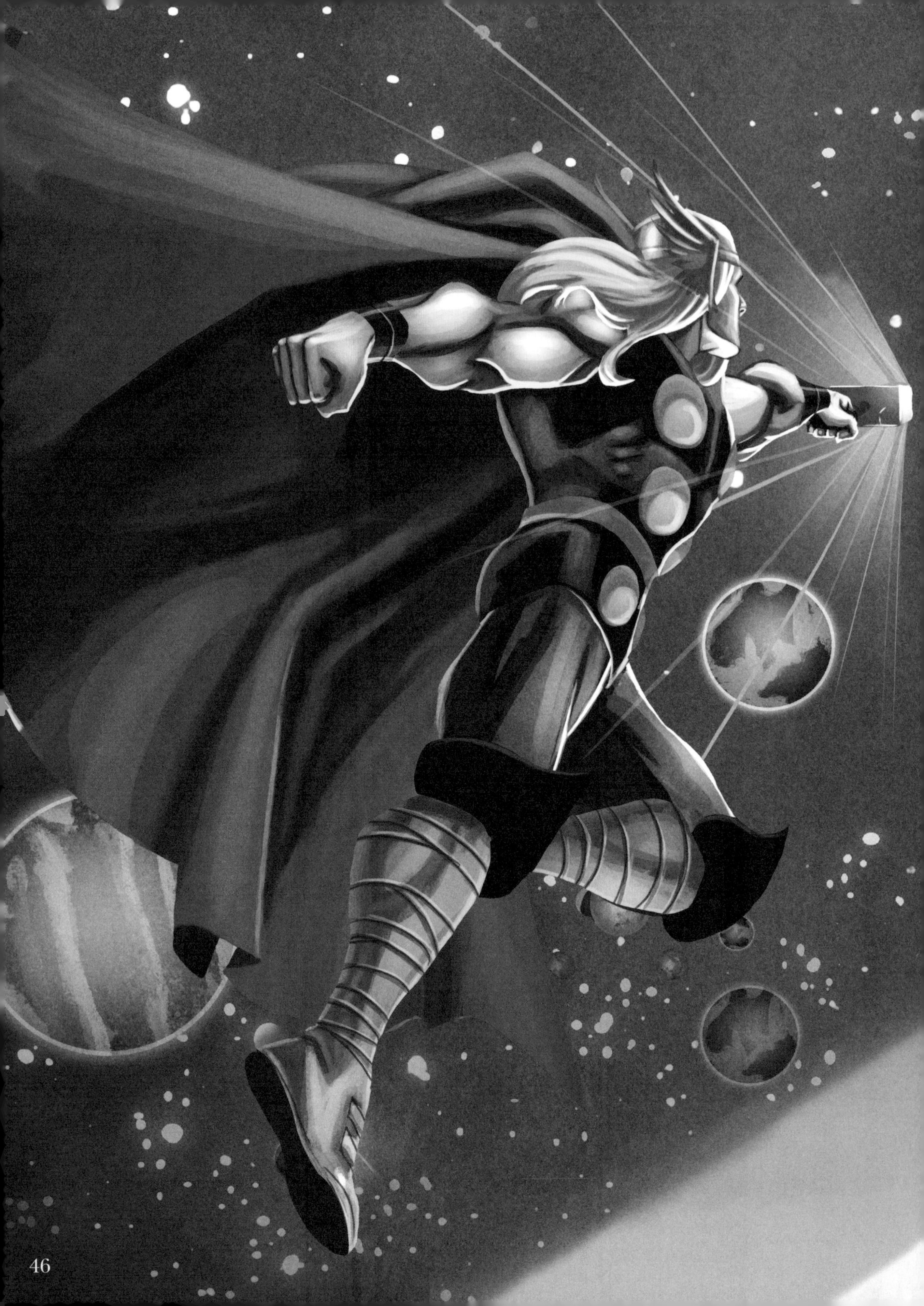

Thor gave Loki a stern look before he left him alone to think about his actions. Thor felt hurt by what Loki had done, but he hoped that one day they could again be the brothers they used to be. He missed his brother. With a heavy heart, Thor spun his mighty hammer and flew off toward the Bifrost.

"This is the perfect place to plot my next plan . . . "
Loki said under his breath as he watched Thor depart.
Loki was no longer the brother Thor knew. He had turned
mad with jealousy and greed. He has forsaken love and
friendship for the promise of power.

As Thor disappeared into the sky, Loki let out an evil
snicker. "Watch out, brother. I'll return for my revenge . . .
and my throne!"

THE INVINCIBLE IRON MAN

Iron Man's New Armor

Tony Stark wasn't pleased with his Iron Man armor. He felt that it made him look too scary to those he was trying to help. He wanted a suit of armor that looked sharp but was also functional. Yes, Tony Stark was the Invincible Iron Man, but he was also a stylish billionaire who loved the finer things in life.

Building the perfect new suit wasn't easy work. Tony made a few versions that were better than the first, but they weren't exactly what he wanted.

When a piece of his suit's armor came off, Tony wasn't discouraged. Instead of giving up, Tony kept going back to the drawing board.

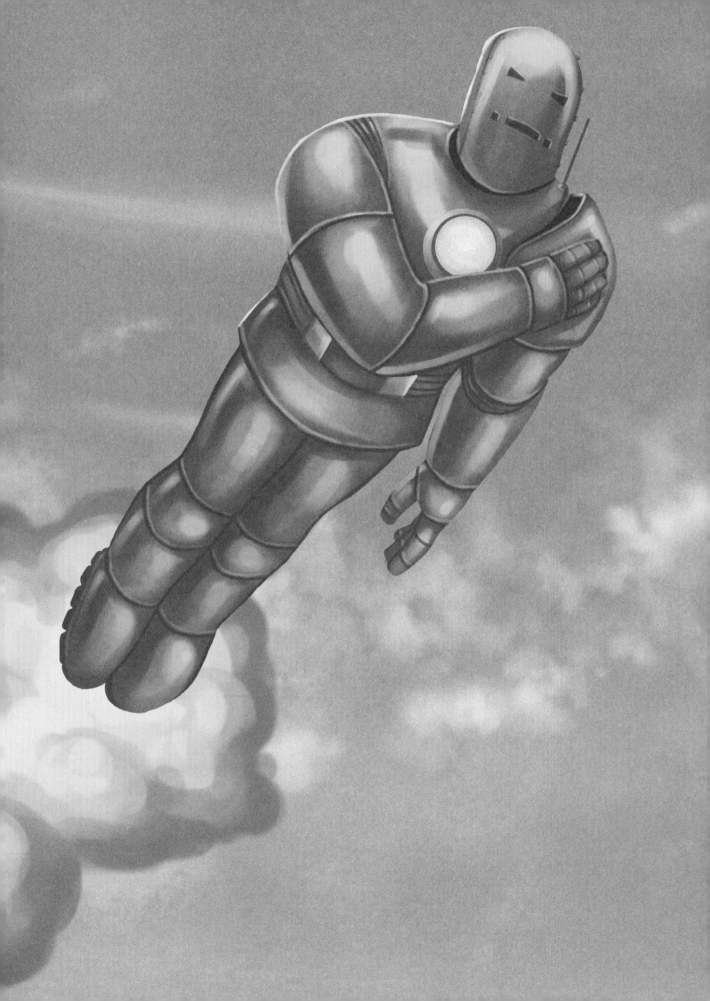

Tony wanted to create the most powerful and amazing suit of armor possible, and he knew that it takes time to make something that good. He also knew that the most important thing was that he not give up. He would keep trying until he made the best armor he could.

After working very hard for many long nights, Tony finally created a lighter suit that also looked very sharp.

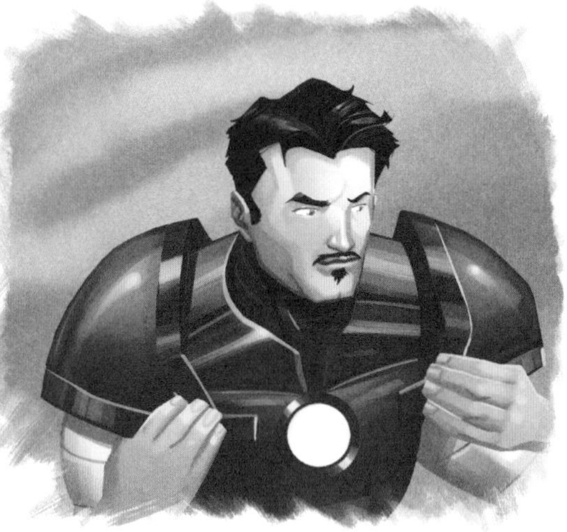
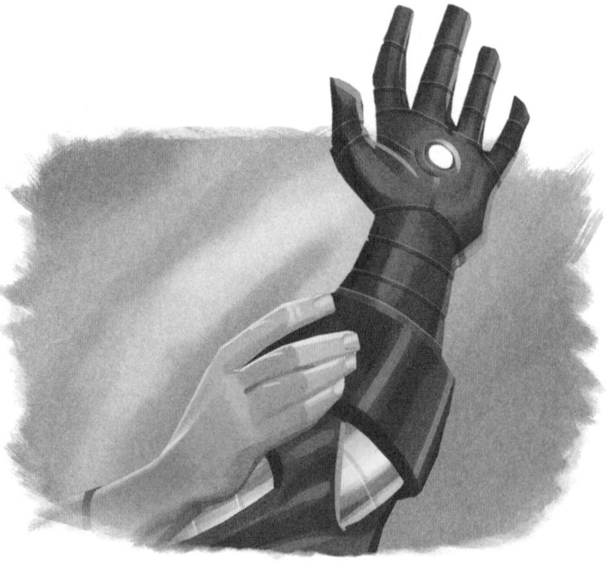
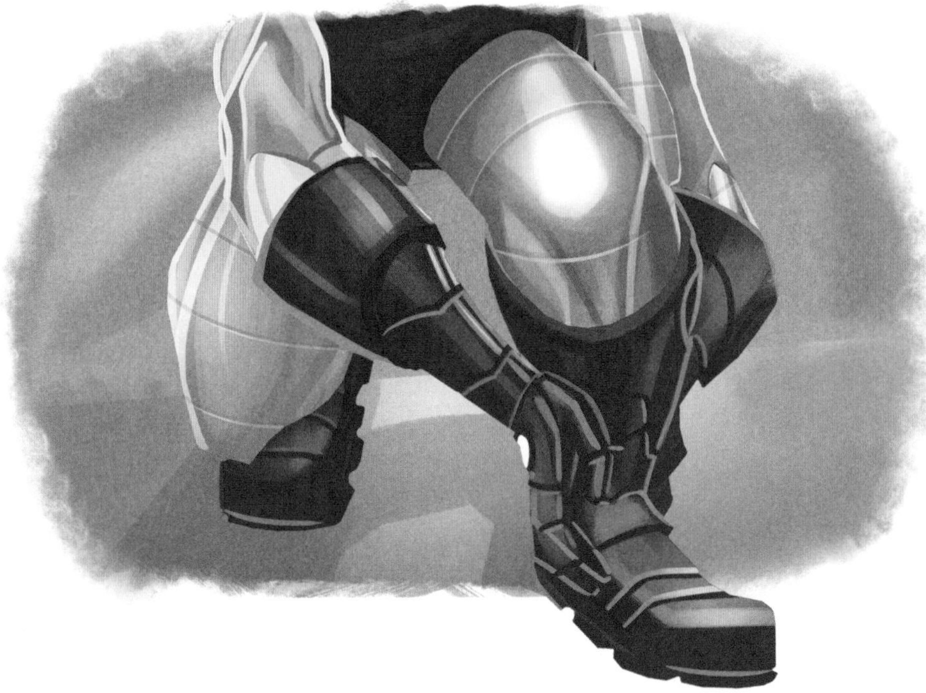
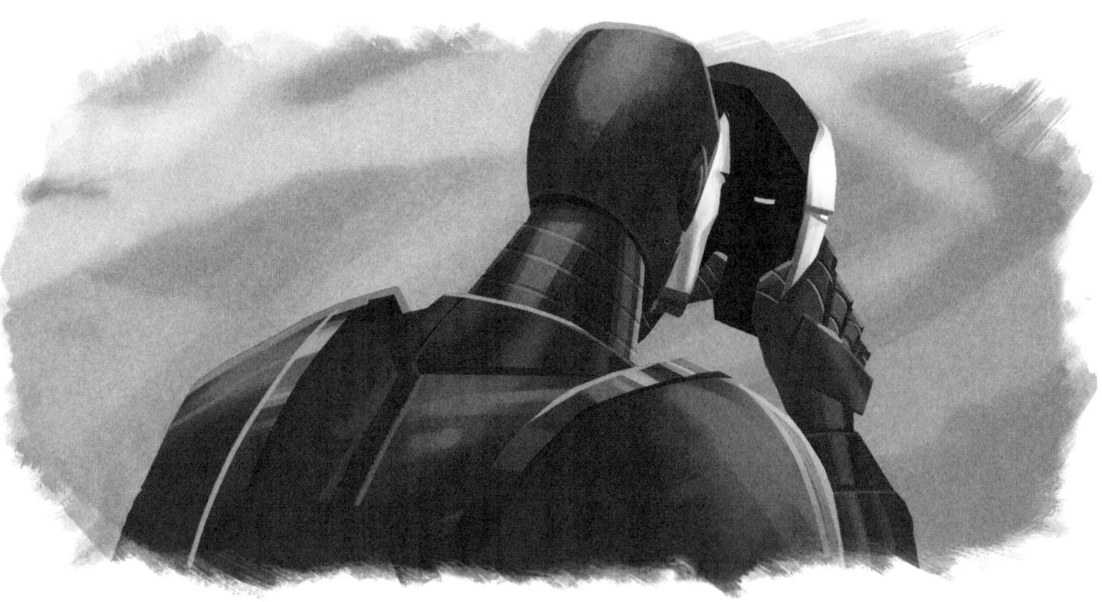

It was red and yellow and had a chest plate to protect his heart. He put on the helmet and was finally the Iron Man he wanted to be. Now he could protect the world and people wouldn't be frightened of him.

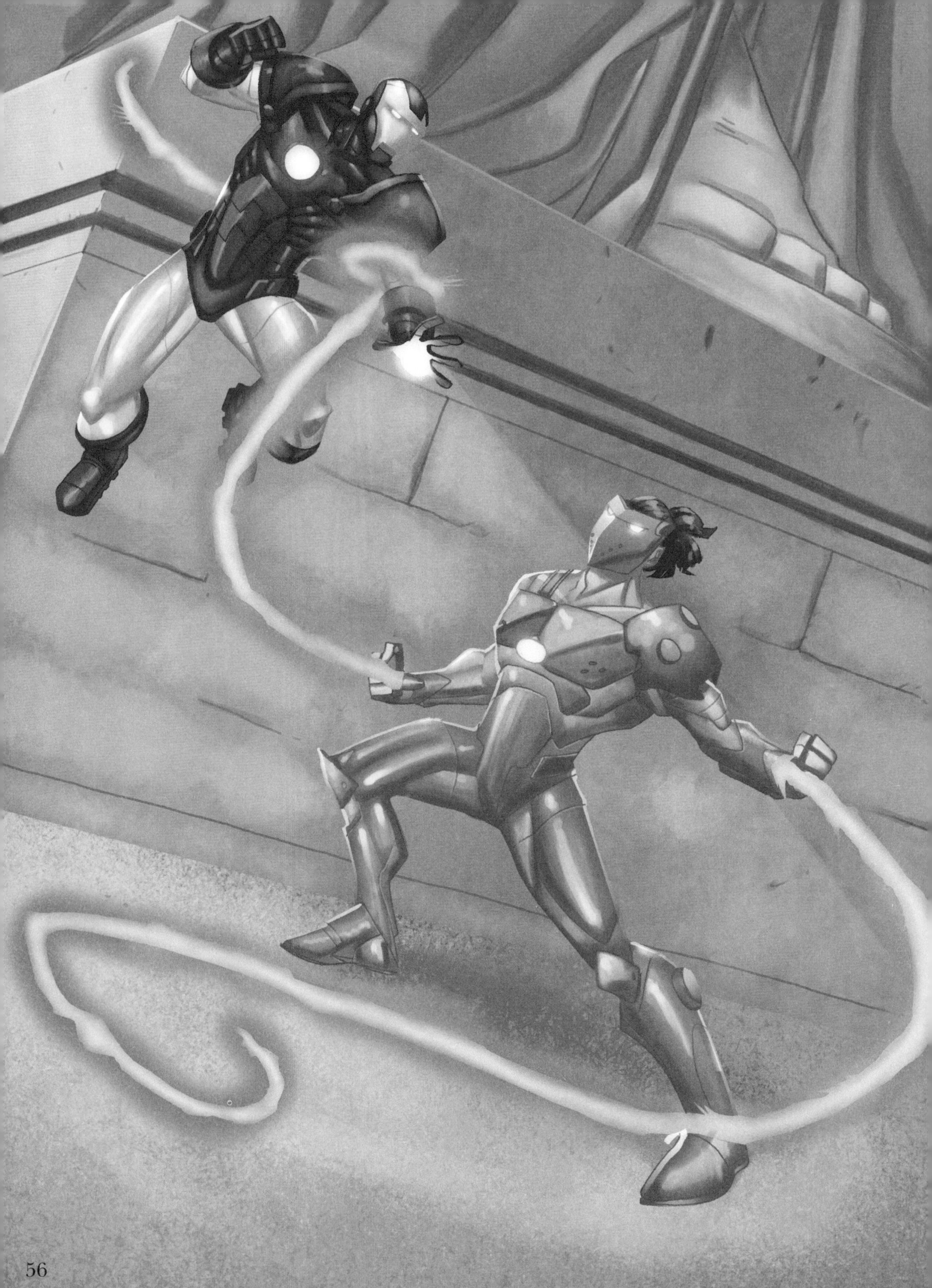

When Tony heard the news that the evil Super Villain Whiplash was attacking New York City, Tony decided to put his new armor to the test.

Iron Man found Whiplash at the Statue of Liberty. The statue stands for freedom, and Iron Man wasn't going to let Whiplash destroy it.

"Stop this attack, Whiplash," Iron Man yelled through his helmet.

Whiplash replied by attacking the Armored Avenger with his electrified whips! They sparked against Iron Man's new armor, and Tony hoped that his new suit would be strong enough to withstand the attack. Iron Man then let out a repulsor ray blast, but Whiplash fought back and blocked the blast with his whips. He was a lot more powerful than Iron Man expected.

Whiplash cracked his whips, sending sparks of electricity at Iron Man. The Armored Avenger quickly fired his rocket boosters and evaded the blasts.

"If you're trying to scare me, you're going to have to do a lot better than that!" Iron Man said as he dodged another attack.

"Admit it, Iron Man," Whiplash shouted. "You are weak, just like the rest of your country!"

Iron Man flew toward Whiplash, grabbed him, and shot straight up into the air. The night sky looked like a lightning storm as Whiplash tried to break free from Iron Man's mighty grip.

"What are you doing?" Whiplash screamed as they rose high above the statue.

"I just want to ask you a question," Iron Man began. "Are you more afraid of heights?" Iron Man mocked. "Or water?"

"No! Put me down," Whiplash protested.

"Are you sure?" Iron Man said. "I'm not sure you want to fall from this height!"

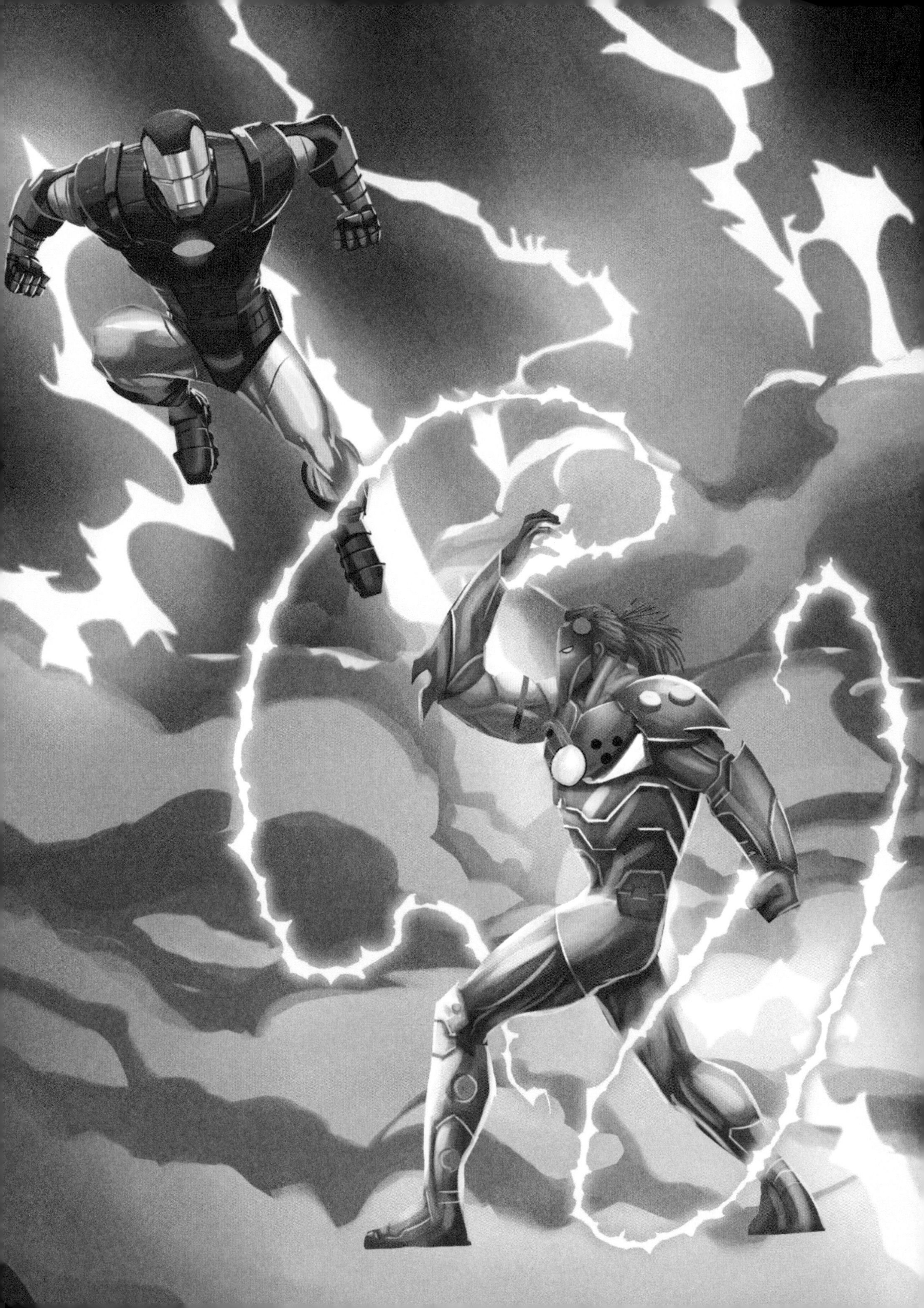

"Fine, I give up," Whiplash said, realizing that if his electric whips touched even a drop of liquid it would be the end of him for sure.

Once they were back on dry land, the police took Whiplash into custody. Iron Man looked at the Statue of Liberty and smiled. Tony Stark was pleased that he was able to stop the attack and test out his new armor. Tony's hard work had paid off.

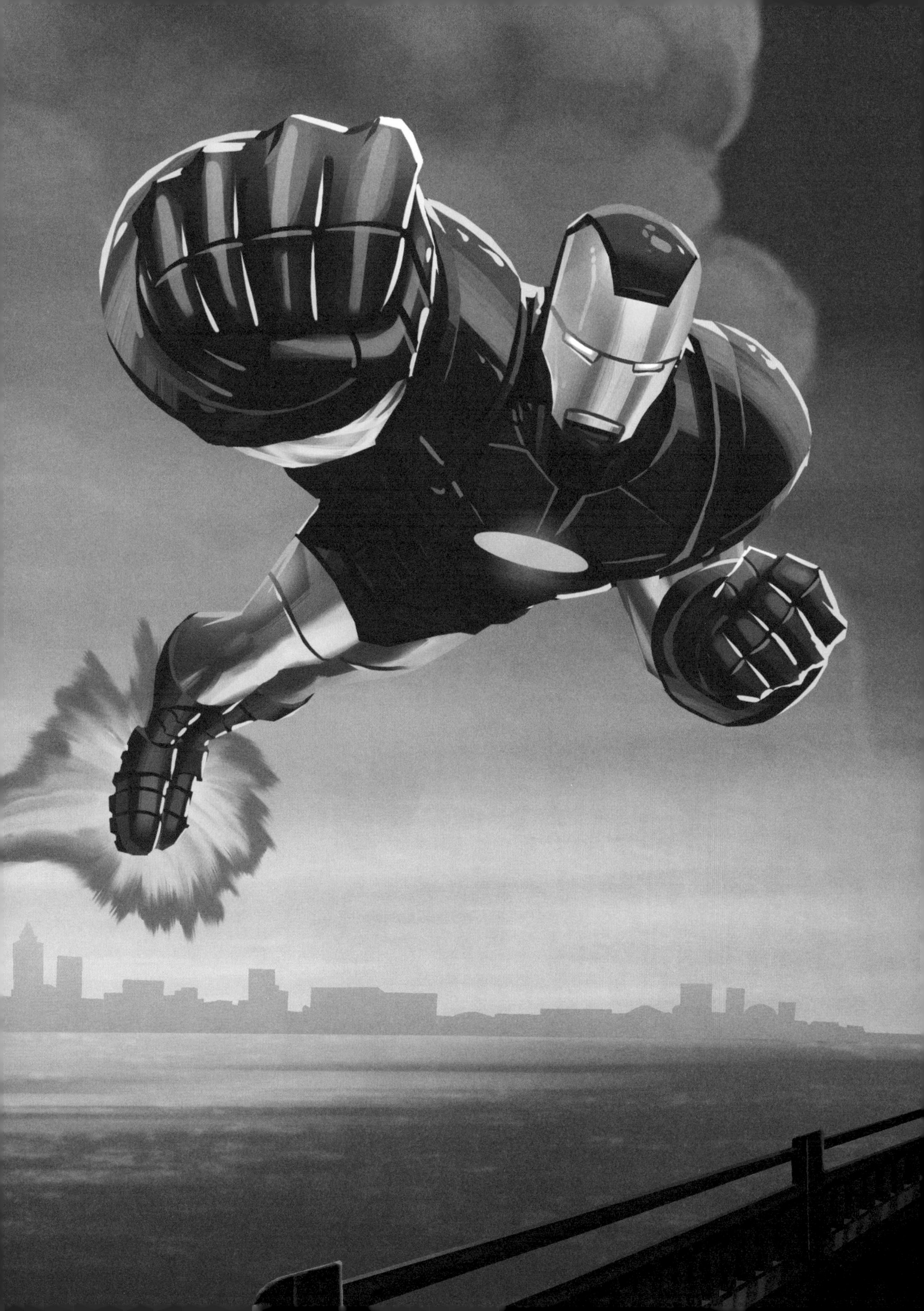

As Iron Man flew through the starry sky with its beautiful full moon, he thought about everything that had happened. And as he soared high above Manhattan, he looked down and knew there were people below who needed both Tony Stark's technology and Iron Man's invincible armor. And that gave Tony—and Iron Man—all the strength in the world!

Spider-Man vs. Sandman

Peter Parker felt invisible at Midtown High. Today was especially hard because his two best friends, Mary Jane Watson and Harry Osborn, were on a drama-club field trip to see a play. They asked Peter to join them, but he had a big science test he couldn't miss. With Peter's friends away, Flash Thompson decided it was a good time to bully him. Flash Thompson was the worst bully in the school, and he wouldn't leave Peter alone. He tried to cheat off Peter when their teacher, Mr. Isaacs, wasn't looking.

Peter daydreamed that the students knew he was really the Amazing Spider-Man, and that they had made posters that read, WE LOVE PETER! He imagined himself being the most popular kid in school.

"Peter," Mr. Isaacs said, snapping him back to reality, "can you show the class how you answered the extra credit question?" But before Peter could respond, a scream rang out followed by a cry for help.

As all the other kids ran to the window to see what was happening, Peter ran to the door. He had to sneak out of class to help!

When he exited the school, he wasn't Peter Parker—he was Spider-Man! And Spider-Man was shocked to see Sandman running down the street. He had to catch the villain before he got away. Sandman was moving fast, so Spider-Man had to move faster. He shot a web and swung high into the sky, landing safely atop a school bus that was headed in the same direction as Sandman.

Spider-Man jumped off the bus and climbed straight up
the wall of a nearby building. He could see Sandman across
the street. It was time to confront the villain!

"Stop it, Sandy!" Spidey shouted. Spider-Man leaped off
the wall and landed hard atop Sandman. But the powerful
Sandman just pushed off the wall-crawler.

The villain laughed as he tried to intimidate Spider-Man with his height. "Outta my way, runt. You'll never beat the Sandman!" Sandman was a bully like Flash Thompson, and he needed to be stopped.

Sandman enlarged his fists and brought them down like two giant sledgehammers. Thanks to his spider-sense that warned him of danger, Spider-Man jumped back just in the nick of time. Sandman was powerful, but Spider-Man wasn't about to give up. Spidey was going to use his smarts to defeat this evil criminal, just like he did with hard math problems at school.

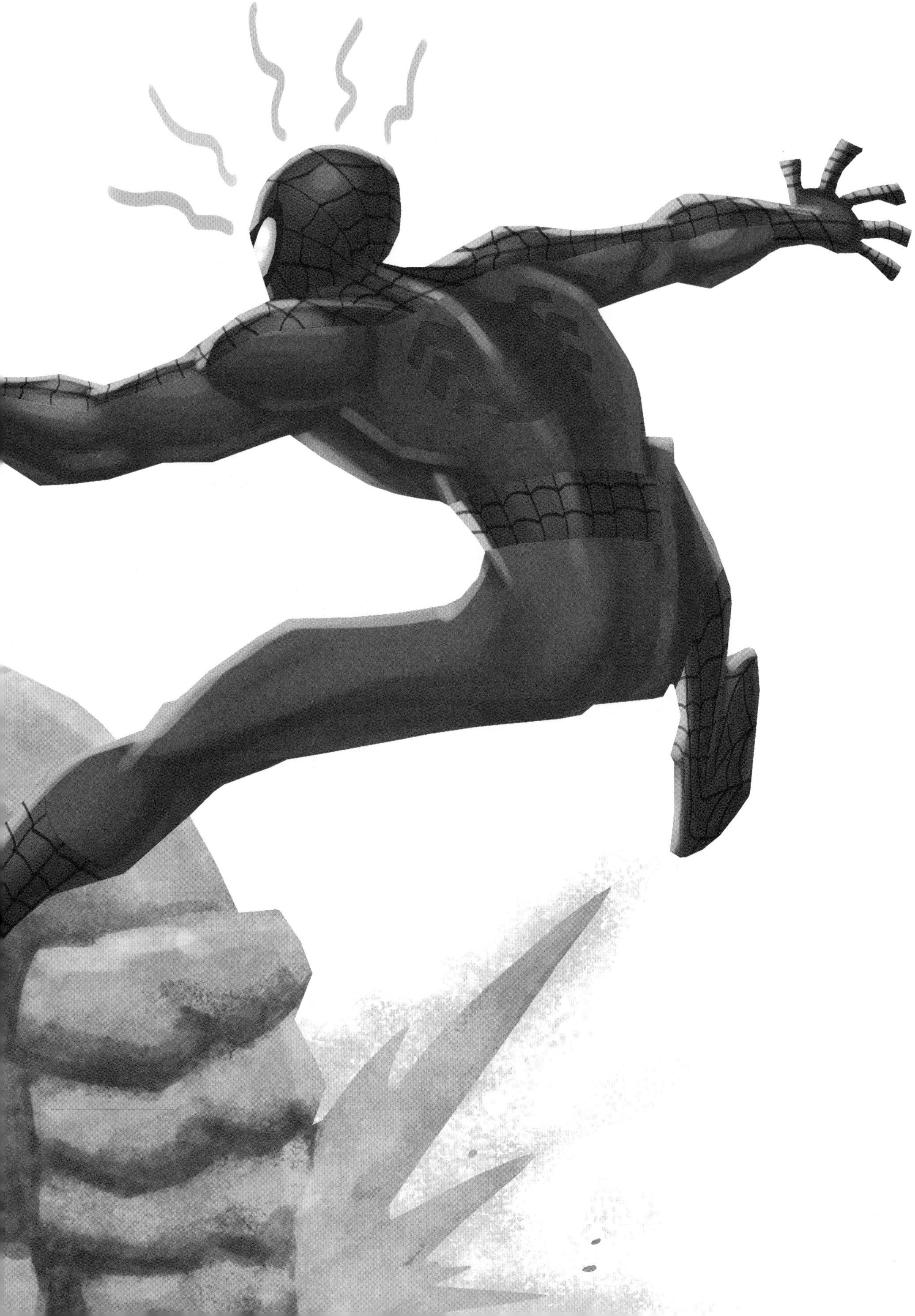

With all his strength, Spider-Man punched Sandman, but the web-slinger's hand went right through the villain's body.

This is going to be harder than I thought, Spider-Man said to himself. This was a tough problem, but he'd solve it.

Sandman knocked Spider-Man to the ground and started to run down the street back toward Midtown High.

"Oh, no!" Spidey yelled. "Looks like I'm going back to school." I can't let the students down, not even Flash Thompson. I've got to outsmart Sandman, Peter said to himself as he raced down the street after Sandman.

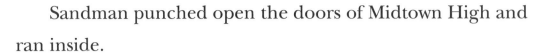

Sandman punched open the doors of Midtown High and ran inside.

"Class dismissed!" Sandman shouted.

"Stop!" a school security guard yelled.

"I don't need a hall pass," Sandman said to the guard as he knocked him out of the way.

"You don't break the rules at school, Sandy!" a voice yelled from behind the vile villain. It was the Amazing Spider-Man!

Students screamed and ran into classrooms, but when they saw Spider-Man was there to save the day, they peeked around almost-closed doors to watch the battle.

Spider-Man saw Mr. Johnsen, the school janitor, and had an idea. He finally knew how to solve this problem. Spidey shot a web-line and grabbed the janitor's vacuum cleaner. He turned it on, then set it as high as it could go and charged at Sandman.

"Look, Sandy, you may be strong, but you're really nothing but a sandbag. Have fun in your new home—the school vacuum," Spidey said as he captured Sandman in the vacuum cleaner.

With the battle over, all the kids ran out of their classes to see their hero, Spider-Man.

Spidey knew none of the students realized that Peter Parker was missing; they were too in awe of Spider-Man and how he saved them from the evil Sandman.

Secretly, Peter wanted to remove his mask and show the school, especially Flash Thompson, who he really was—but he didn't. As Uncle Ben always said, "With great power comes great responsibility." Peter knew that keeping his identity a secret was the best way he could fight criminals like Sandman—and protect Aunt May.

As all the students surrounded Spider-Man, nobody knew that Peter had a big smile underneath that mask. Peter was happy to have helped them, and that was all that mattered.

THE INVINCIBLE IRON MAN™

Surprise Attack

Tony Stark was ready for the busy day ahead of him. With Pepper Potts's help, Tony found a nice tie to wear for today's meeting with Victor Wong, one of the biggest businessmen in the United States. Tony was very excited to discuss Stark Industry's new technology and inventions with Mr. Wong. This was a very important meeting!

But as Tony took a sip of his coffee, he almost spit it back out! Not because it tasted bad or was too hot, but because when he looked up from his mug, he spotted something outside his window. There was a large, robotlike villain attacking a building! It was Crimson Dynamo!

Quickly, Tony took out a secret briefcase from under his desk and unlocked it. Inside was his famous Iron Man armor. He called Pepper.

"Pepper, tell Mr. Wong I'm going to be running late . . ." Tony said.

"What? You can't be late for this meeting! It's with Victor Wong, the president of M.O., Inc." Pepper panicked.

"Unfortunately, I'm in the middle of something right now," Tony said, staring at his own reflection in the Iron Man helmet. He knew it was his duty as Iron Man to stop Crimson Dynamo and protect innocent civilians.

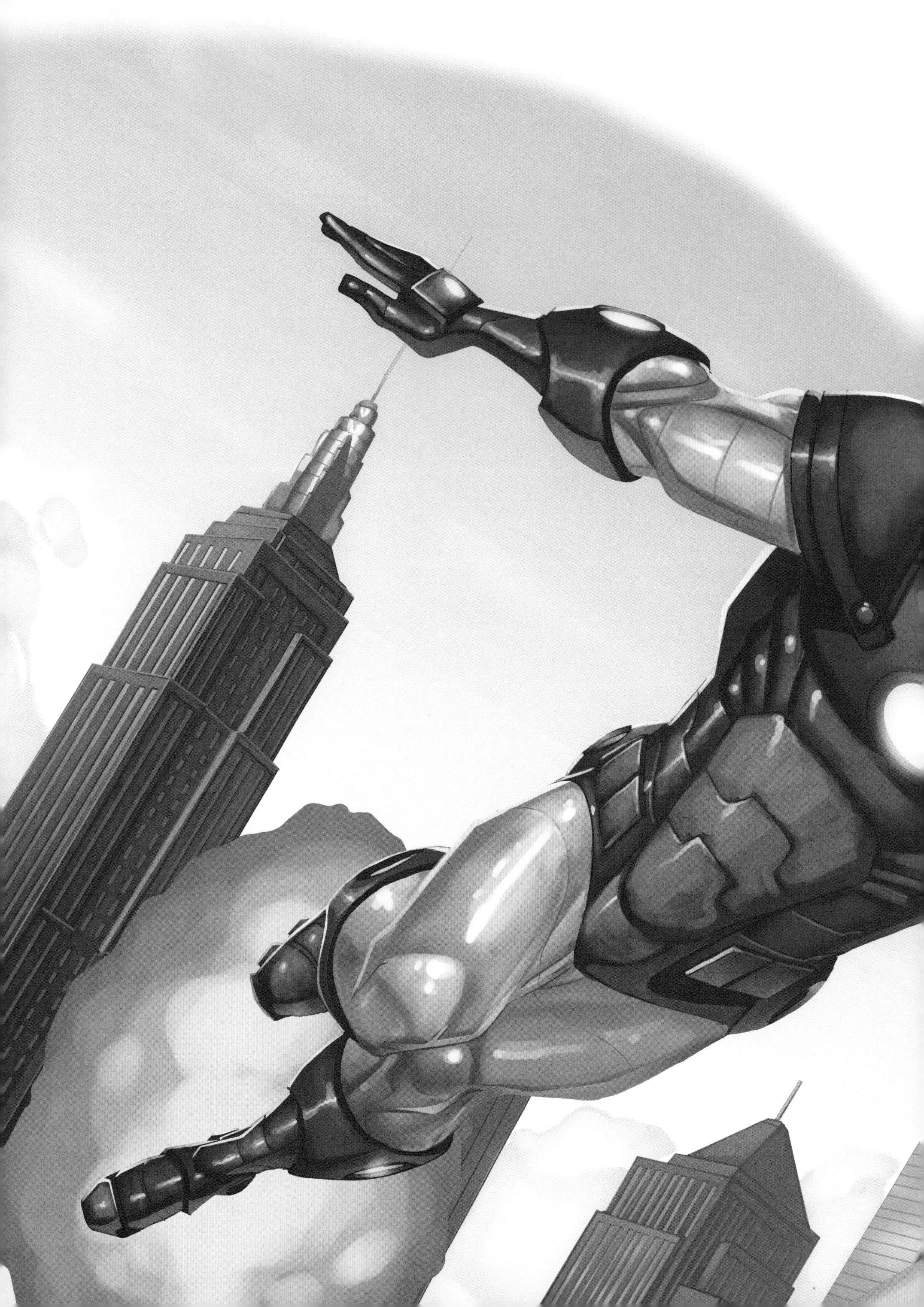

Shooting off into the sky, Iron Man felt ready for whatever Crimson Dynamo might throw at him. But he could feel his stomach starting to turn a little. Tony hated to admit it, but sometimes even Super Heroes could get a little nervous about a big meeting . . . let alone being late for one. Instead, he focused all his energy on defeating Crimson Dynamo. He flew toward the evil Super Villain, ready for action.

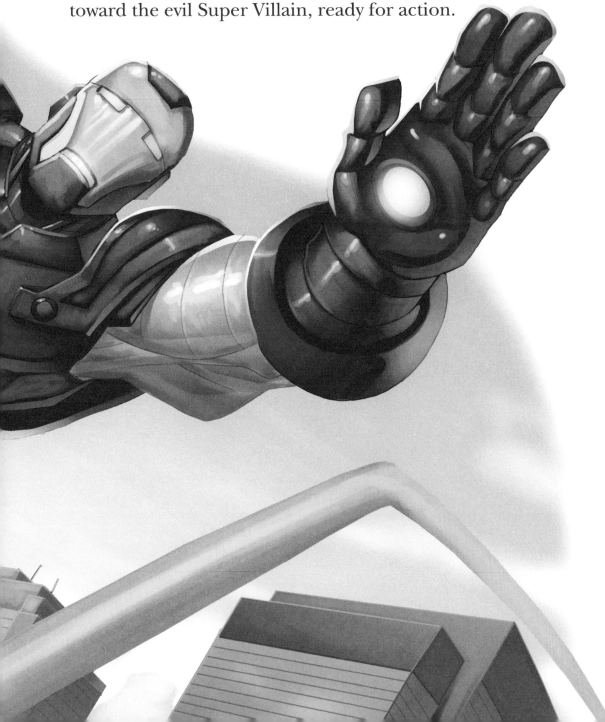

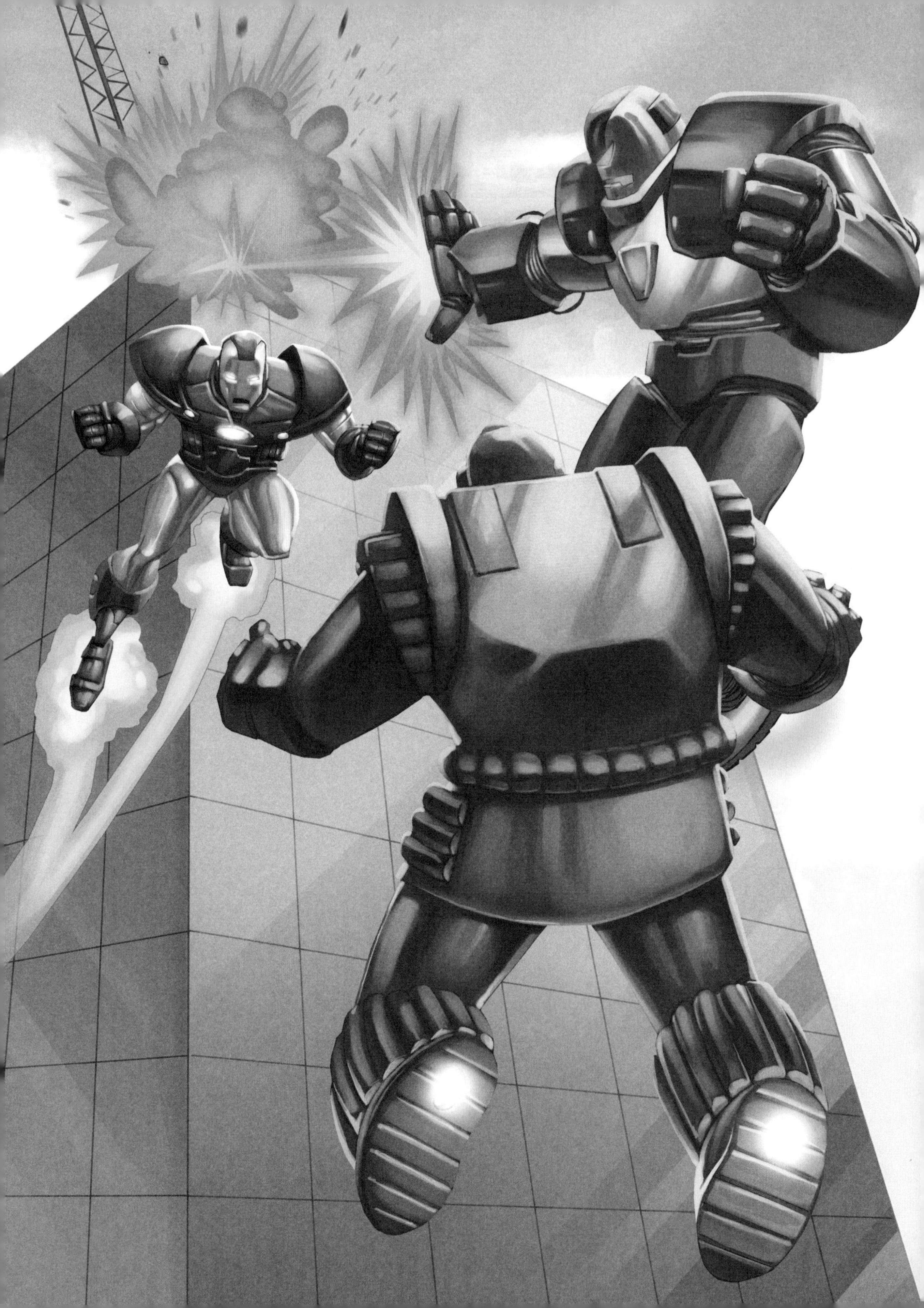

As Iron Man approached the giant villain, it seemed like Crimson Dynamo was expecting him . . . and so was Titanium Man! Iron Man was caught by surprise! Crimson Dynamo was causing mayhem in front of Stark Tower purposely to get Tony's attention and bring him right into a trap set by not one but two Super Villains!

Tony wondered what these thugs were up to. He knew they enjoyed stealing his inventions for their own evil purposes. Crimson Dynamo, eager to get the first shot at the Super Hero, immediately aimed his weapon at Iron Man. Luckily for Tony, the villain missed and got the Stark Tower's antenna instead.

"Hey, you better pay for that! Not like the technology you stole from me," Iron Man yelled.

"So Iron Man has come out to play," Titanium Man said.

"What about a game of tag?" Iron Man asked. Swiftly, the Armored Avenger fired a repulsor blast at Titanium Man! "Tag! You're *it*!"

Iron Man dashed off behind a building. The crooks quickly followed. Glancing back, Iron Man was not sure how he was going to take on two Super Villains at the same time, but he needed to get these thugs away from the people inside the buildings and watching from the streets below.

"We don't want to play hide-and-seek with you!" Crimson Dynamo yelled, clearly frustrated.

"We want the new Stark Industries technology you invented! Come and fight like a real Super Hero—if you even are one," Titanium Man shouted.

While the two villains were busy looking for Iron Man, they did not notice Tony sneaking up behind them.

"Didn't your mother ever teach you to say please?"
Iron Man interrupted them. "And as a matter of fact, you
can't have my new inventions, because I'll be presenting
them in my meeting today—which you're making me
late for!" The two thugs were shocked to see Iron Man
behind them.

"Now it's my turn to count to ten!" Iron Man shouted.

Instantly, the Invincible Iron Man raised his arms, aiming his repulsors directly at the two Super Villains.

"One . . . two . . . ten! Ready or not, here I come!" Iron Man yelled. Before they knew it, Iron Man shot his powerful repulsor blasts at full force! It looked like Iron Man might be able to stop Crimson Dynamo and Titanium Man *and* be back in time for his meeting! But then, Crimson Dynamo started to get back up!

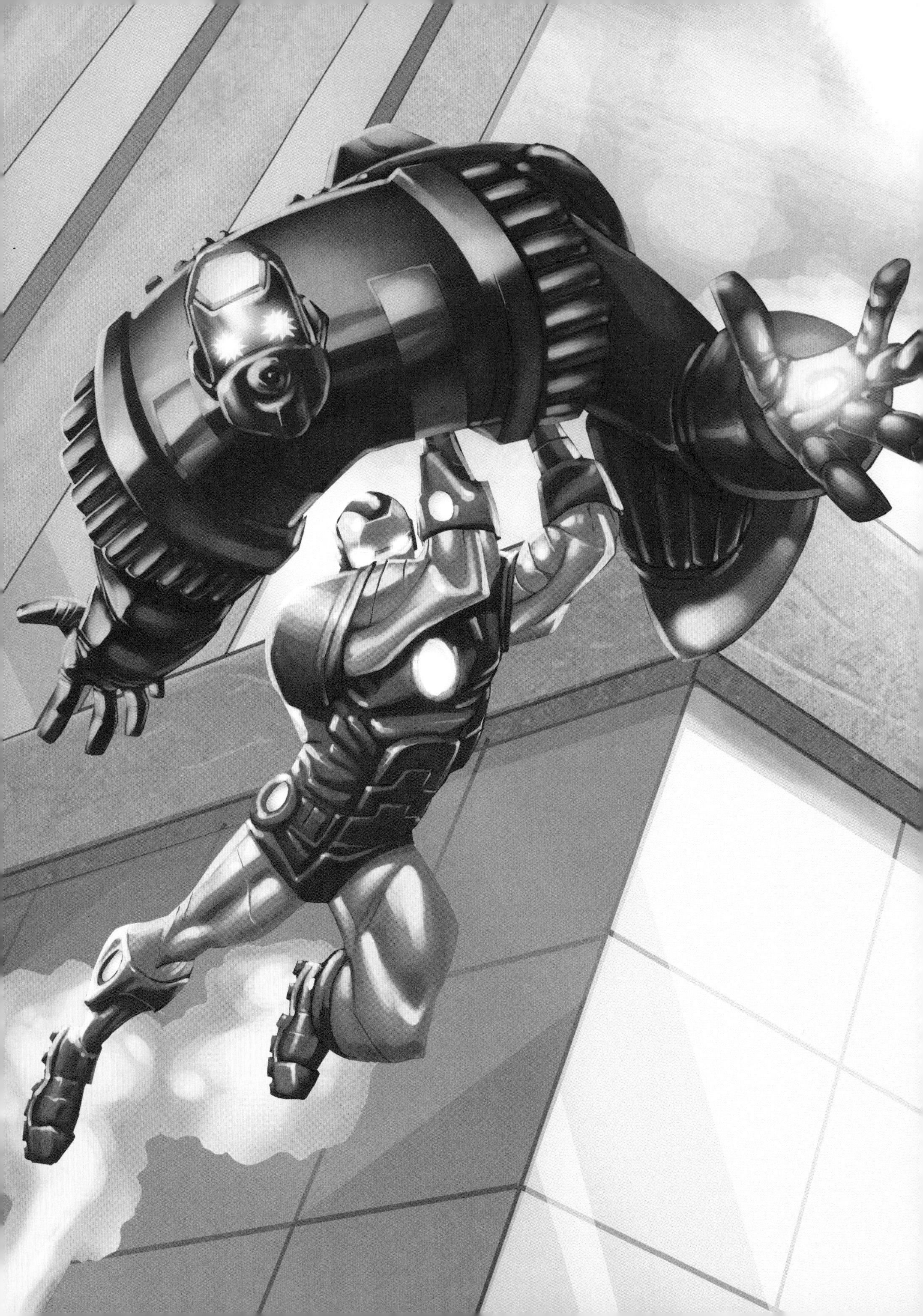

Tony immediately increased his power levels to three hundred percent! Then, Iron Man grabbed hold of Titanium Man and lifted him high above his head. Titanium Man tried to fight back but was completely powerless!

"Let me go!" Titanium Man whined. But Iron Man ignored him and shot up, up, up, until he was higher than any skyscraper, still holding on to the metallic menace.

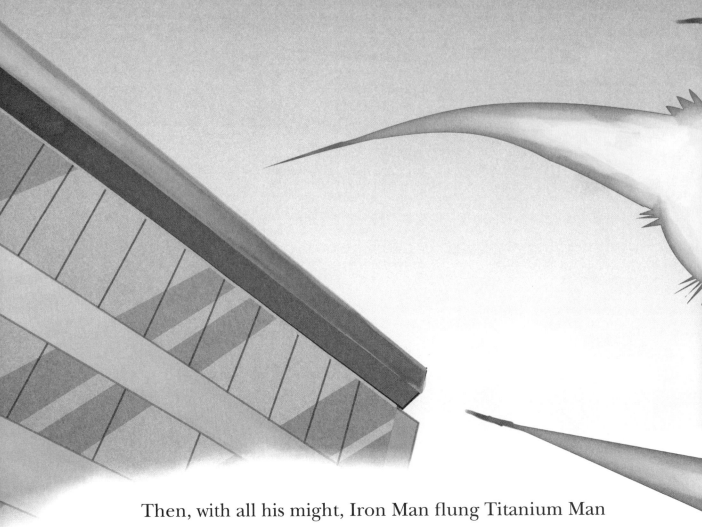

Then, with all his might, Iron Man flung Titanium Man down at Crimson Dynamo, knocking them both out at the same time!

"I got a strike!" Iron Man joked, watching the two Super Villains fall helplessly to the ground like bowling pins. The police were already at the scene to arrest them.

"Now, if you boys would excuse me, I have a meeting to attend," Iron Man said.

Iron Man rushed back to his office and took off his helmet. He glanced at his clock. It looked as if he would be on time for his meeting after all!

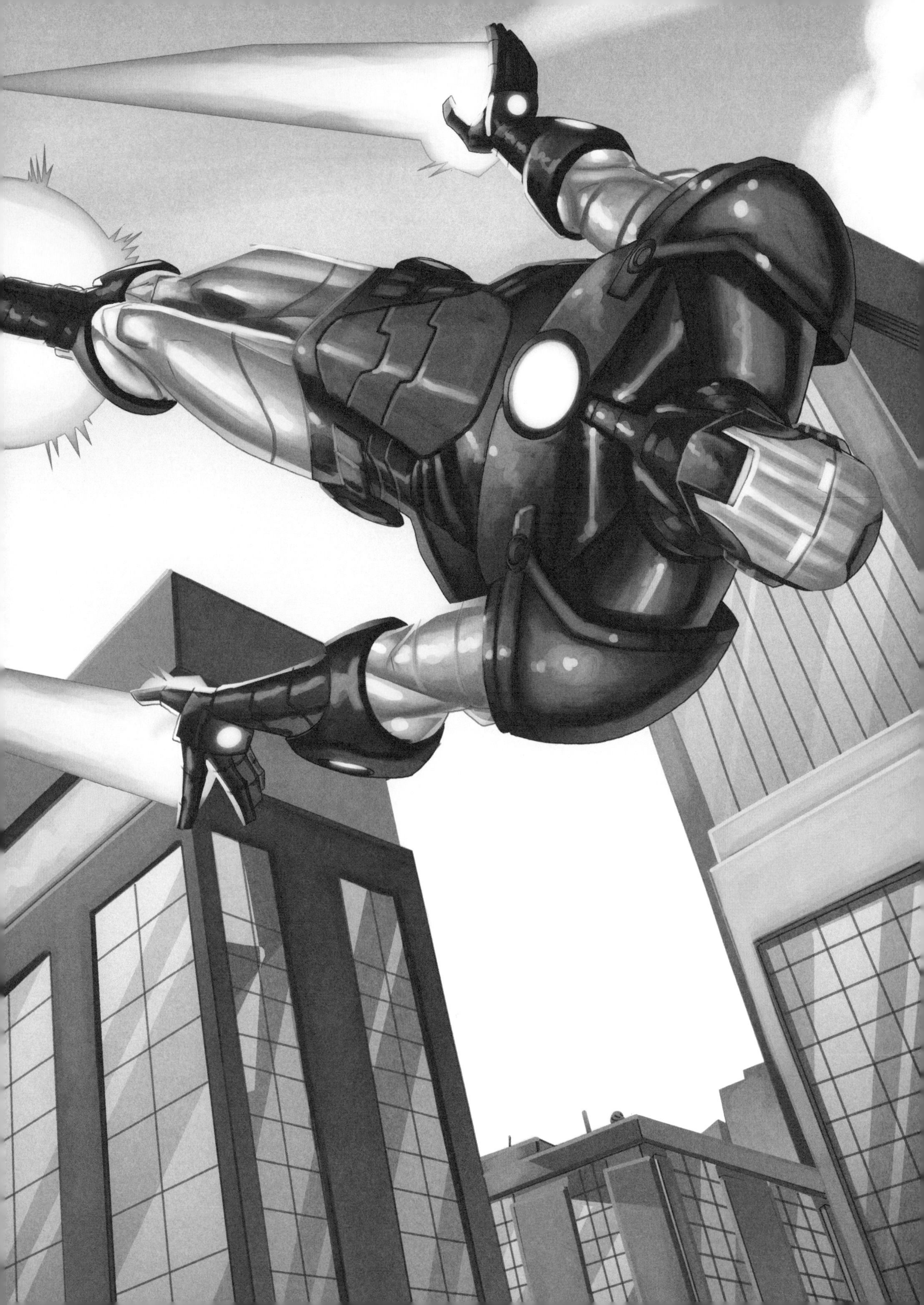

"I guess I'll have to make do with helmet hair," Tony said to himself as he tried to fix his hair.

The jitters he was originally feeling were long gone. If the Invincible Iron Man could handle two giant Super Villains, then Tony Stark could definitely handle one big boss. Tony smiled confidently to himself. All in a day's work for a billionaire businessman—and the Invincible Iron Man!

Captain America Returns

The Mighty Avengers were in the Arctic Sea when they first saw Namor. They heard rumors that the legendary Super Hero and king of the underwater city of Atlantis had returned, and they were excited to finally find him. Namor hadn't been seen on land in decades.

"Atlantis is in ruins!" Namor yelled as he approached the Avengers. "The humans must have destroyed it. Because of that, I will take my revenge on all of you!" Namor said as he leaped toward the heroes.

The Avengers quickly realized Namor was no longer a friend. After Atlantis was destroyed, he must have become an enemy, and now they were forced to battle him.

"Revenge will be mine!" Namor shouted as he punched Iron Man across his metal jaw.

Iron Man was shocked by Namor's strength, but he wasn't going to give up. Neither were the other Avengers.

Earth's Mightiest Heroes knew Namor's powers came from water. Since they were near the sea, this would be a challenging fight.

Namor knocked Ant-Man onto the ice, then quickly came up from behind Thor to attack him, too. Just then, the Incredible Hulk used all his strength to deliver a mighty blow to Namor, instantly sending the king of Atlantis a hundred feet away.

But the Avengers couldn't let Namor escape, so they jumped in the Quinjet and followed the Sub-Mariner into the icy depths of the Arctic. Suddenly, Iron Man spotted something floating in the water. Ant-Man left the craft to investigate and discovered that it was a man frozen in a block of ice.

Ant-Man brought him into the sick bay and Iron Man used his repulsor rays to warm the ice, freeing the man. The Avengers were stunned at what they saw—they had just rescued the famed Captain America!

The Avengers stared at Captain America in awe! Captain America was the ultimate hero and Super-Soldier. He had been lost at sea during the Great War, but now Captain America had returned.

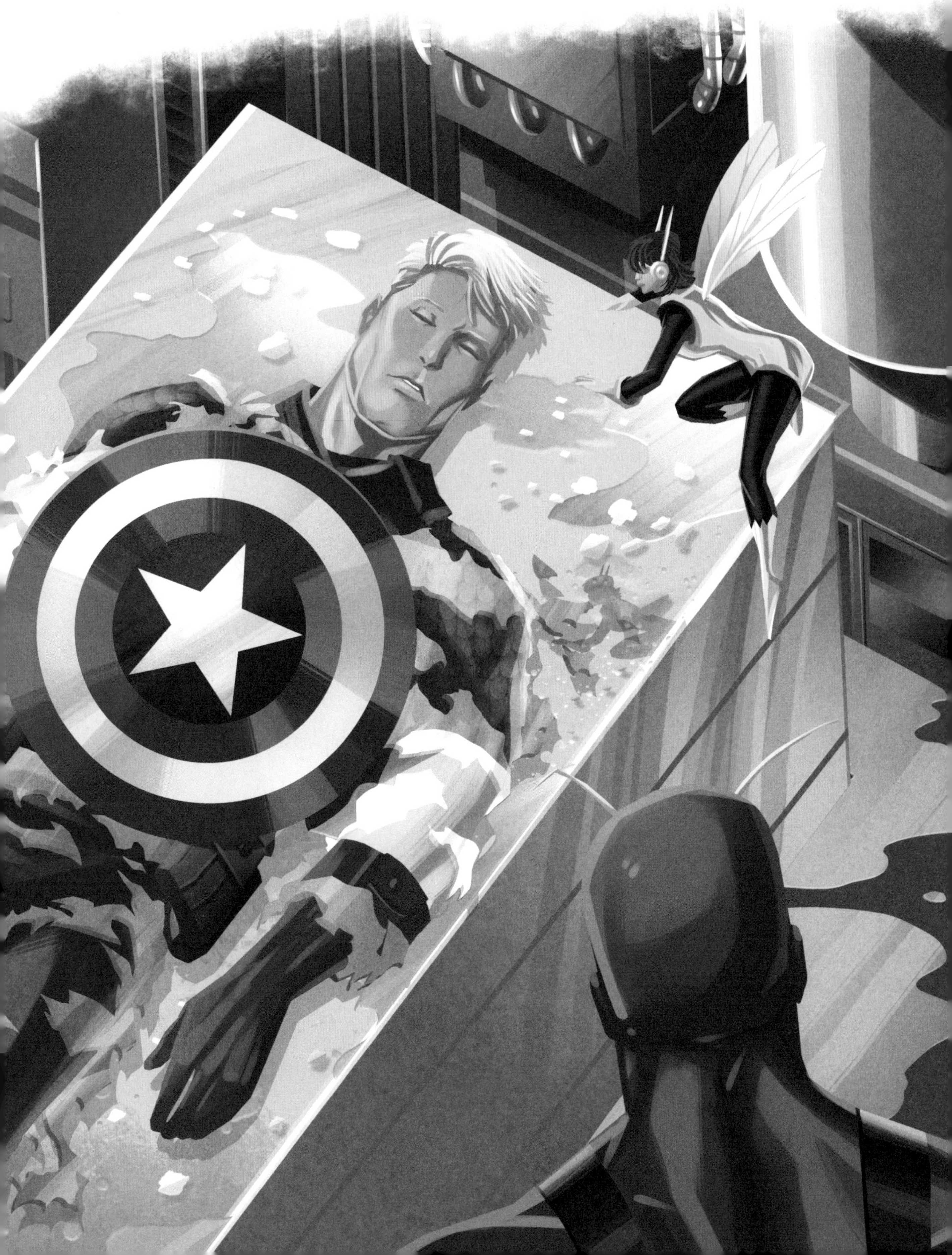

"Do you know who you are?" Thor asked when Captain America woke up. Cap was alarmed at first and didn't know where he was.

"I think so," replied Captain America.

"You are one of America's greatest heroes, Cap," Wasp said. "It's been a long time since the world has seen you. They missed you."

"I feel so tired," Captain America said.

"The ice must have put you in a deep sleep where you didn't age," Iron Man said. "It might take you time to adjust, but I'm sure you'll be back to your old self very soon."

Iron Man showed the lost hero around the Avengers'
Quinjet. Captain America slowly began to learn about
the modern world. He had never seen any of the gadgets
the Avengers had on their ship, and he had to learn how
to use them.

When Captain America figured out how to turn on the TV, he saw an image of Namor on the screen. Cap couldn't remember who this person was, but he seemed familiar.

Suddenly, something rocked the Quinjet, startling the Avengers and throwing them all off their feet. It was Namor. He had returned for his revenge, but this time he brought the Atlantean army with him.

NEWS 4   HAS THE SEA KING RETURNED?

RK INDUSTRIES POSTS GAINS · RICHARDS CONFIRMS SH   IGLAIN P

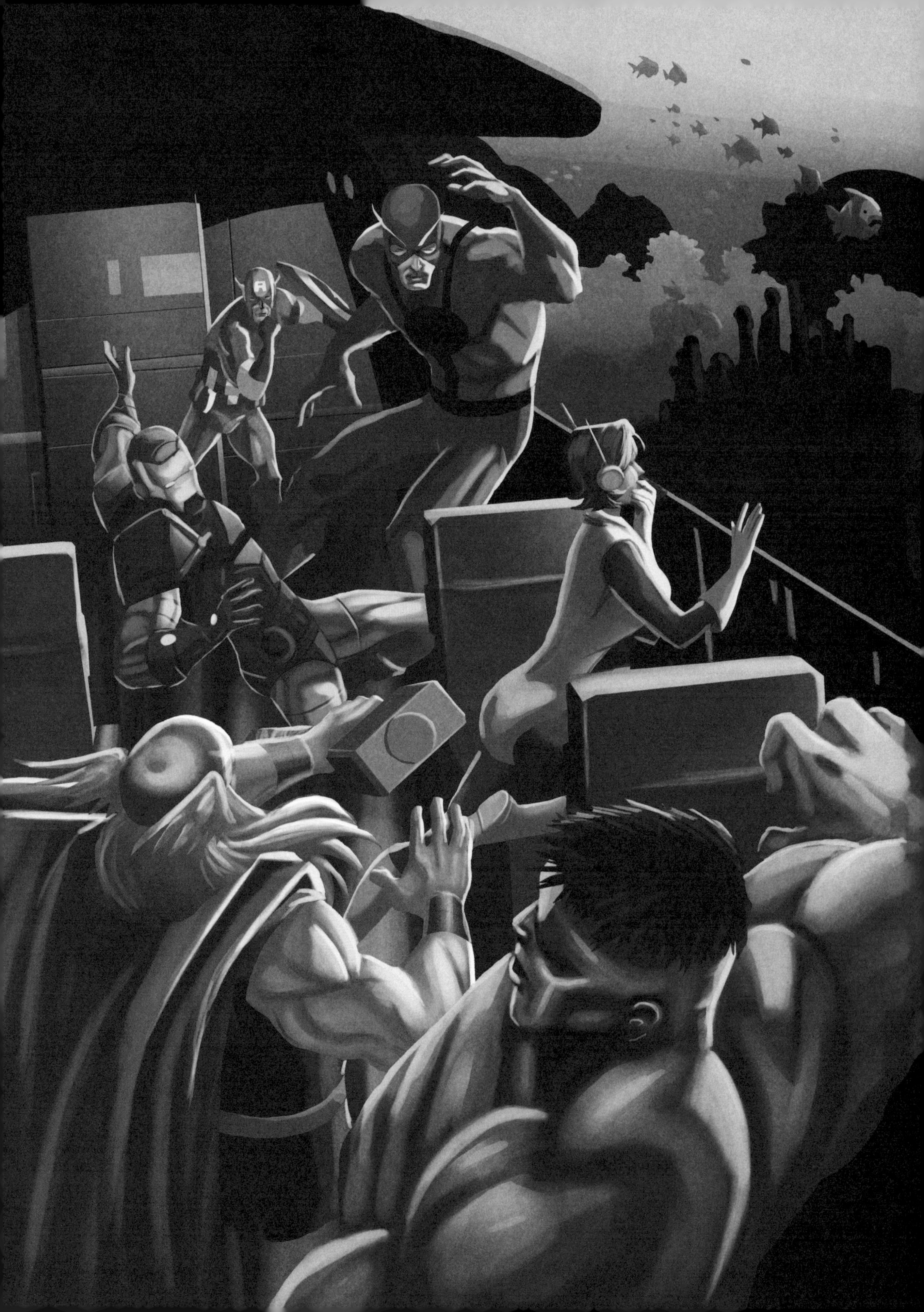

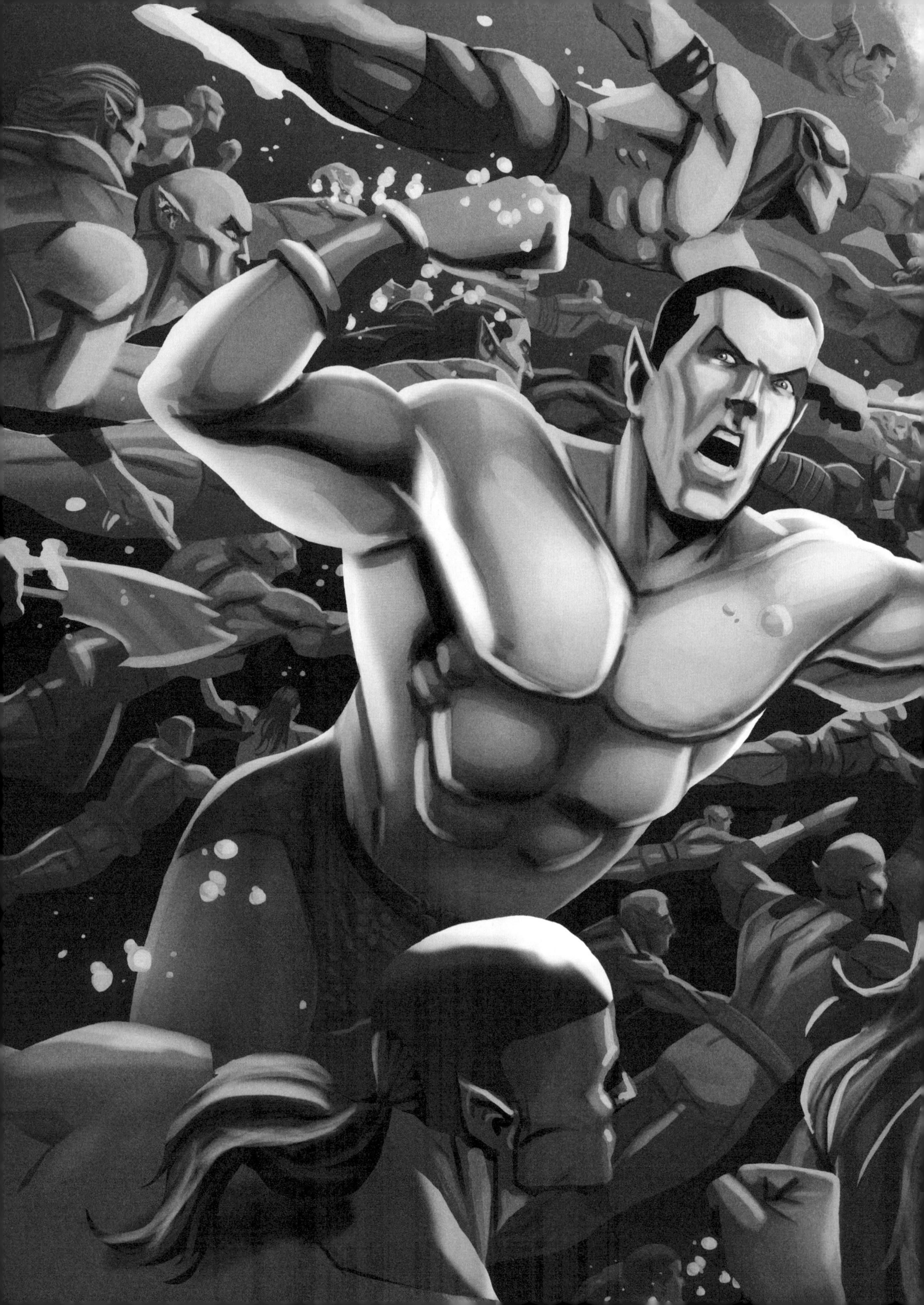

From the window of the Quinjet, the Avengers could see an armada of Atlantean soldiers swimming toward them. They were outnumbered!

Like Namor, the Atlantean army became more powerful in water, and the Avengers had to get to land to weaken them. It was their only chance.

The Avengers raced to land and fought long and hard, but there were just too many Atlanteans. Not even Earth's Mightiest Heroes could stop them all!

And then, just as the battle appeared to be lost, a Super Hero who wasn't an Avenger stepped in. A red, white, and blue blur whizzed past the Avengers, knocking down one Atlantean after another. The Avengers realized it was a shield—the shield of the Courageous Captain America!

Now that Captain America was helping them, they could win the battle. Thor used his mighty hammer to defeat a battalion of Atlantean soldiers while Iron Man, Ant-Man, and Wasp fought against Namor and his men. Together, they were able to drive off Namor and his entire army! Cap and the Avengers knew they could not have done it alone.

The Avengers had a new member that day. Captain America had joined those who had saved him from the ice, and now Earth's Mightiest Heroes were even mightier—and the people of the earth were even safer—thanks to Captain America and the Avengers!

Spider-Man vs. the Sinister Six

Peter Parker had just dropped off some photos at *The Daily Bugle* when a special bulletin ran across the television in the newsroom.

"This just in!" the news reporter blared. "The evil group known as the Sinister Six has taken over Lower Manhattan! Spider-Man! If you are out there, we need your help!"

But Peter was already out the door. This looks like a job for your friendly neighborhood Spider-Man, he said to himself as he changed into his famous red-and-blue Spidey costume.

Spider-Man swung high above the streets of New York City at great speed. I have to stop the Sinister Six, he said to himself. I've fought each member before, but never all of them at the same time! I'll have to be extra careful if I want to take each one of them down. And that's when it hit Spider-Man—to defeat the Sinister Six, he'd have to fight each member one at a time!

Spider-Man was downtown in minutes and soon met with his first challenge. Just down the street were two large cats circling a man who wore a lion's pelt.

Kraven the Hunter, Spider-Man said to himself. Last time we met, he didn't have his cats with him. This isn't going to be easy, he thought.

Spider-Man swung down and tried to surprise Kraven from behind. But his leopards heard the wall-crawler and leaped right at Spidey!

"Whoa!" Spider-Man cried, barely dodging their sharp claws and snarling jaws.

"Spider-Man! Haven't you learned you can't sneak up on a hunter?" Kraven said as he commanded his beasts to attack Spider-Man again. But this time the web-slinger had a surprise for them. Spider-Man shot webbing that covered both cats with a giant net. Holding tight, Spidey swung the webbed cats around and around and tossed them directly at Kraven!

"Argh!" Kraven cried, as the weight of the leopards knocked him to the ground.

"What's the matter?" Spidey said as he swung away. "Cat got your tongue?"

Spider-Man didn't have to go far to meet the next member of the Sinister Six.

"Electro!" Spidey cried.

"I'm shocked you remembered me!" Electro said as he fired several bolts of electricity directly at Spider-Man!

But Spidey was fast and leaped out of the way just in time! Surprised at how fast Spider-Man was, Electro tried to fire another bolt of electricity, but Spider-Man quickly leaped toward the villain and landed a mighty blow to his jaw.

"Seems like you've lost your spark, Electro," Spider-Man joked as he swung off to find another member of the Sinister Six.

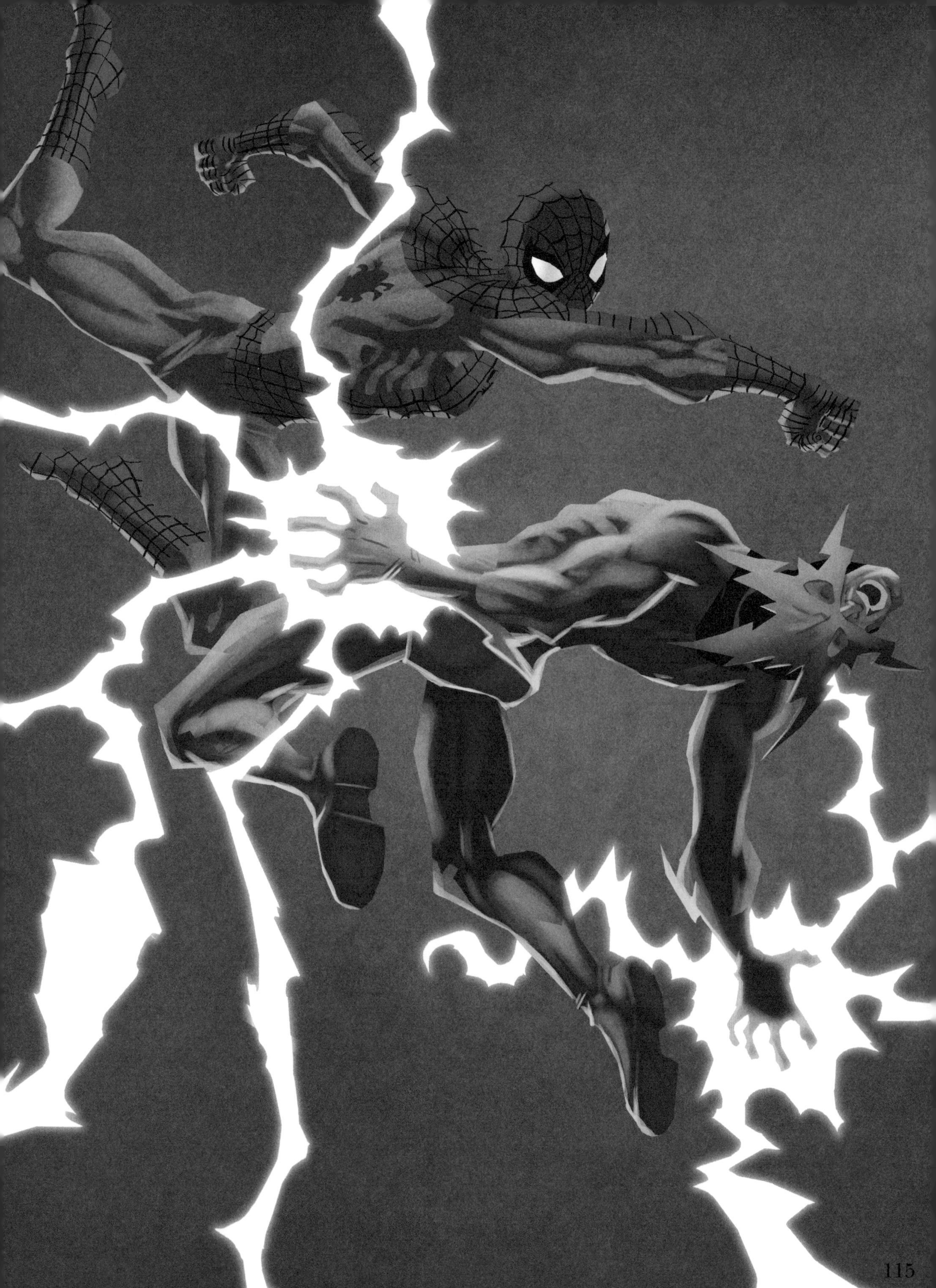

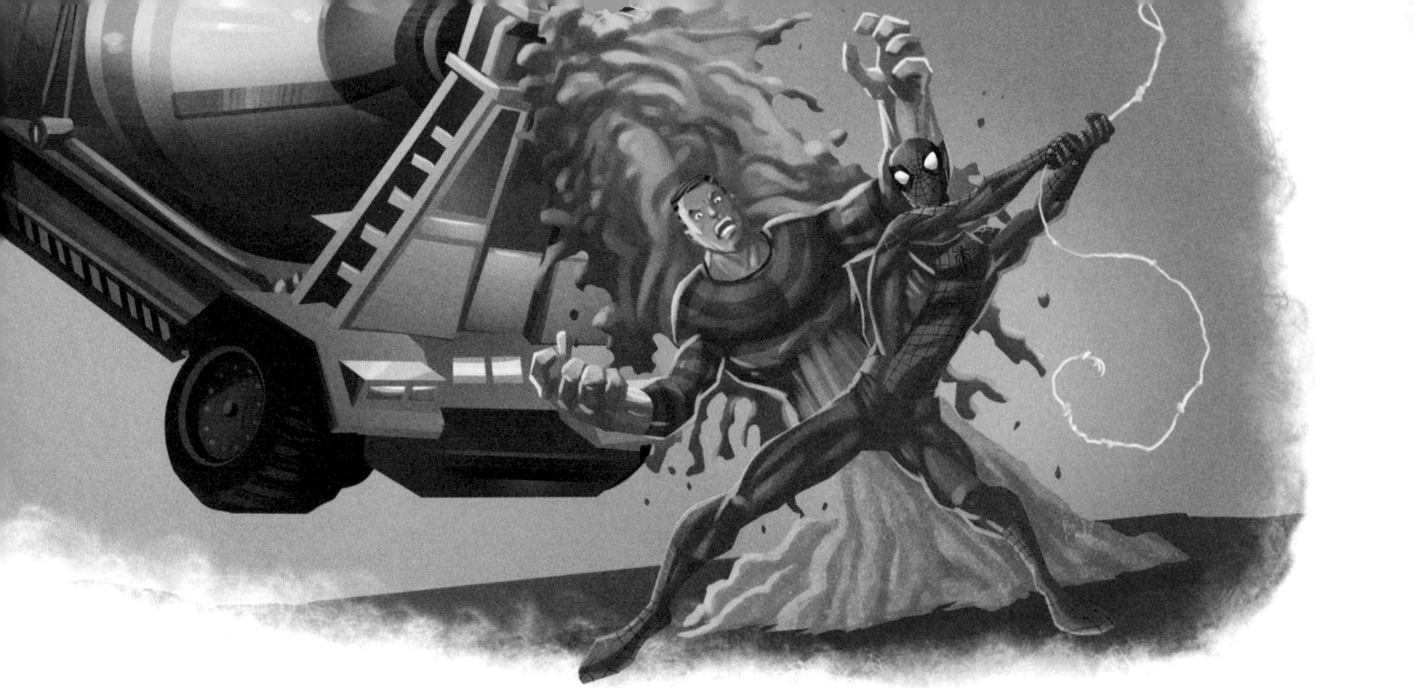

Next, Sandman tried to trap the wall-crawler in quicksand, but Spidey outsmarted him. He covered Sandman in cement and stopped him dead in his tracks! Suddenly, the Vulture swooped down from the sky and slammed into Spider-Man from behind!

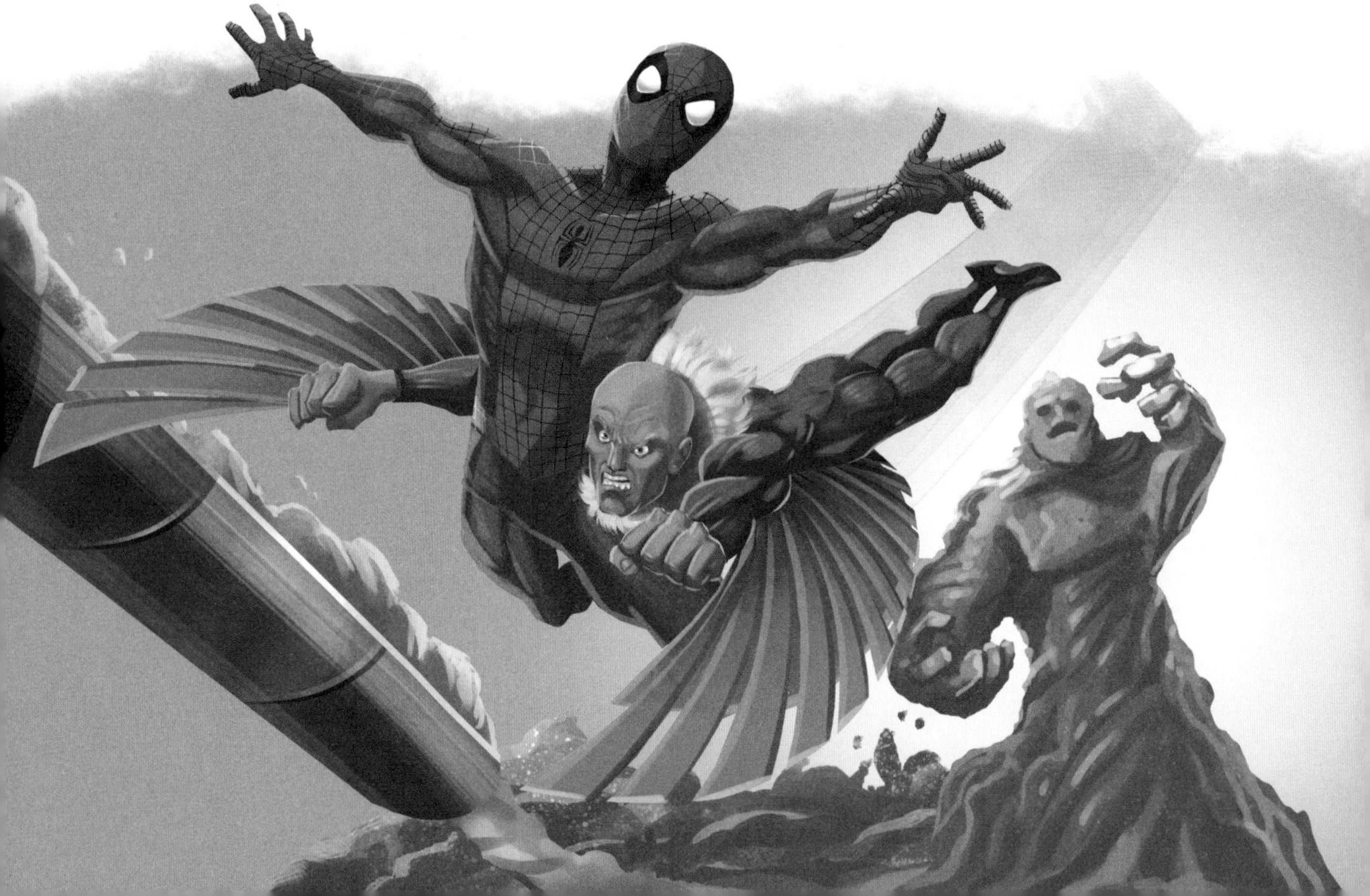

"Do not mess with the Sinister Six, boy!" the Vulture said.

But Spider-Man had already flipped behind the Vulture, webbed his face, and started to ride the villain like a bull!

"And do not hit someone from behind, old man!" Spidey replied.

Spider-Man landed on a nearby rooftop and scanned the area for another member of the Sinister Six, when suddenly something hit Spider-Man—hard!

"What was that?" Spider-Man said, rubbing his head.

"Not *what* was that," replied a mysterious figure behind a cloud of smoke. "*Who* was that!"

"Mysterio!" Spider-Man cried as the master of illusion stepped out from behind the smoke.

"I have waited a long time for this moment," Mysterio said as he hovered over the fallen hero. "You always thought you were better than me! But now the world will see that Mysterio is better than Spider—argh!" Before Mysterio could finish, Spider-Man clobbered Mysterio and sent him flying through the air!

"Did anyone ever tell you that you talk too much?" Spidey said as he dusted himself off. "Maybe your next magic trick will be to make your voice disappear."

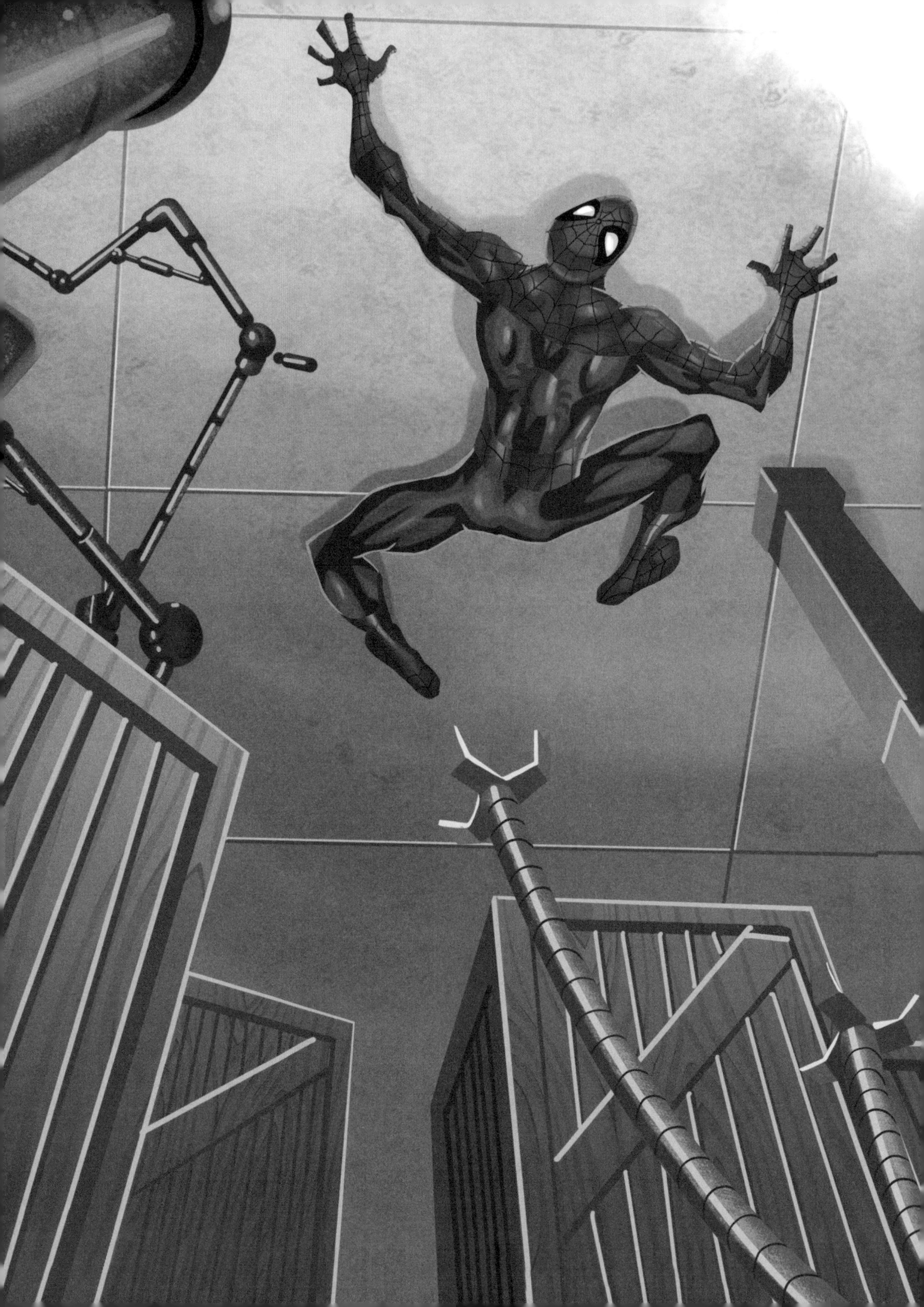

Spider-Man had fought and beaten every member of the Sinister Six except one. And he knew just where that last one was hiding. Spidey saw a mechanical arm slither into an abandoned warehouse across the street. Just as Spider-Man entered the building, his spider-sense went off! He quickly turned to see a mechanical arm striking down in his direction, barely missing him!

"Doc Ock," Spidey said as he rolled out of the way and leaped up onto the ceiling.

"You know an octopus has more legs than a spider," Doc Ock said as his robotic arms thrashed all around him, ready to strike. "And I am about to use mine to destroy you once and for all!"

"Actually, spiders have eight legs, too, Doc," Spider-Man said as he fired several webs at Doc Ock's feet. "Now it's time to get you back in the water!" Spidey said as he yanked on his webs and knocked the mad scientist off his feet.

"No!" Doctor Octopus cried as he fell into a large water tank that was nearby.

"Oh, yes," Spidey said, watching the doctor's arms short out and stop working.

"So," Spider-Man said to the captured Sinister Six, "what have we learned here today? Sandman? Vulture? Kraven? Anybody?" Spider-Man placed his hands on his hips and shook his head. "Being a villain gets you nowhere! Now say it with me: *crime doesn't pay. . . .*" But the villains just moaned in defeat.

"Sorry to run, but I have a date with a meatloaf," Spider-Man said as police cars started to show up at the scene. He leaped into the air and swung off toward Aunt May's house. But before he left, he looked back and laughed. "You guys should stick around for a while. . . ."

Hawkeye and the Mighty Avengers

Sometimes, the world's greatest heroes come from the simplest of beginnings. One example is Clint Barton, better known as Hawkeye—the world's greatest archer and a member of the Mighty Avengers!

Clint and his brother, Barney, were raised in an orphanage. Their lives weren't perfect, but they had each other.

When they were teenagers, the Barton brothers got jobs with a traveling circus. It was at the circus that Clint first picked up a bow and arrow.

The circus's two top acts, who called themselves the Swordmaster and Trick Shot, realized that Clint had the potential to be the best archer ever. Clint decided to call himself Hawkeye, because he could hit any target, no matter how far away it was. Before long, he was the star performer in the circus!

As he got older, Hawkeye eventually ended up leaving the circus and heading out on his own. One day, while performing in New York City, he saw something he had never seen before. A real-life Super Hero! There had been an accident on a Ferris wheel, and Iron Man flew in to save the day!

Hawkeye was inspired by Iron Man's heroics and made himself a Super Hero costume. I bet I could help people, just like Iron Man, he thought. I may not be able to fly or shoot beams from my hands, but I know I can do more than just perform for people.

Growing up in a circus had made Hawkeye a master of more than just the bow and arrow. He had spent years working and playing in the big tent. He could climb ropes, walk a high wire, and do acrobatics just as well as he could hit a bulls-eye.

One of his first nights patrolling the city, Hawkeye
stopped a burglar from robbing a jewelry store. But the
cops thought Hawkeye was the bad guy! Before Hawkeye
could explain that he was innocent, the Invincible Iron
Man appeared overhead. "Is there a new costumed villain
in town?" Iron Man asked.

Iron Man tried to knock over Hawkeye with his repulsor blasts, but Hawkeye used his lightning-fast reflexes to dive out of the way. He knew he had to buy some time to explain himself. He fired a smoke-bomb arrow at Iron Man, followed by an arrow with a special electromagnetic net.

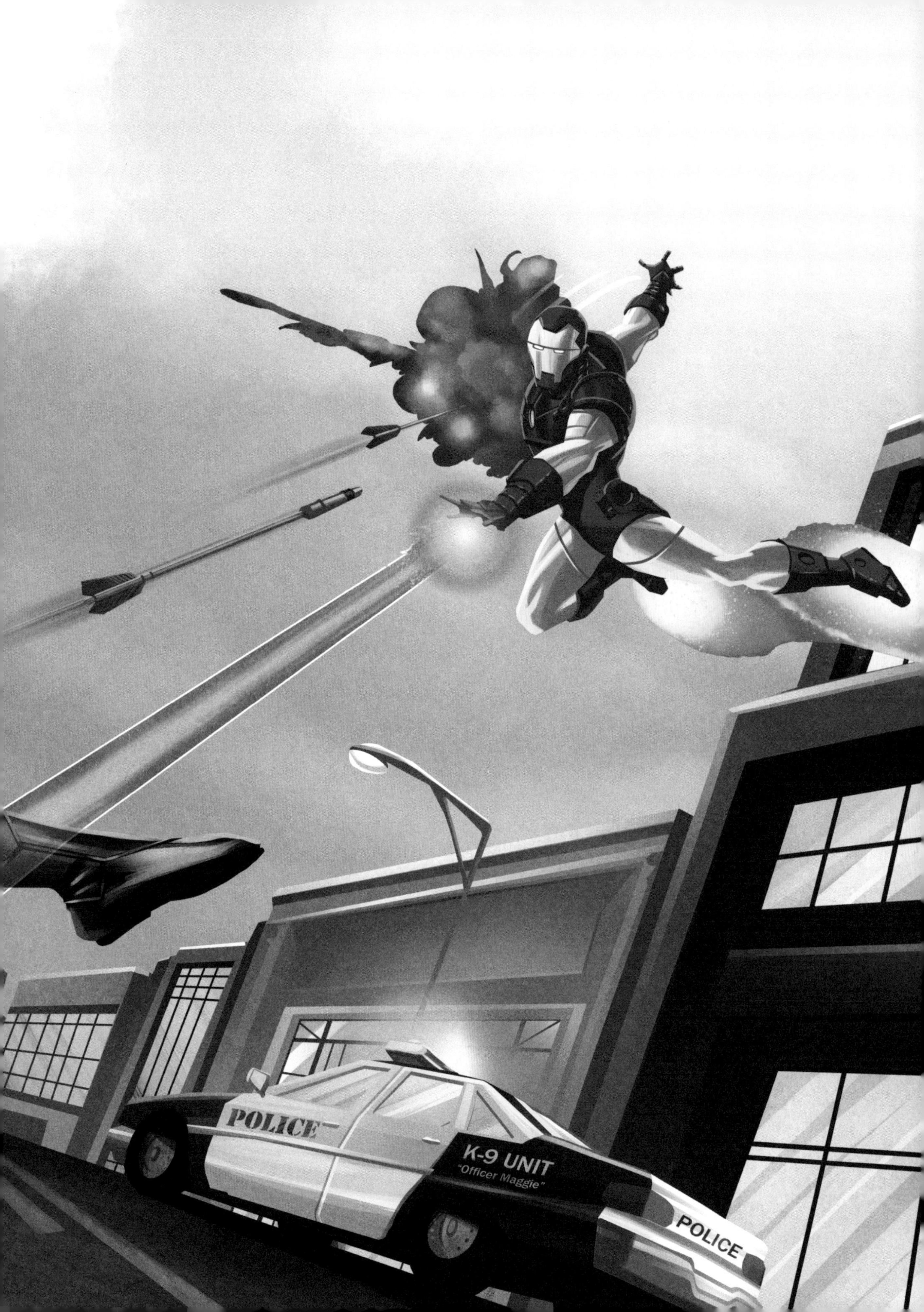
POLICE
K-9 UNIT
"Officer Maggie"
POLICE

Hawkeye's special arrows forced Iron Man to the ground. Hawkeye quickly introduced himself. He told Iron Man how he caught the real thief.

"Well, you certainly are full of surprises," said Iron Man. "I've seen a lot of heroes in action," the Armored Avenger said, "and you've got skills like I've *never* seen before. How'd you like to meet some of my friends?"

Before Hawkeye knew it, the rest of the Mighty Avengers had joined them. Captain America, Thor, the Hulk, Black Widow, Wasp, and Ant-Man—the Earth's Mightiest Heroes! And what happened next was something Clint would never forget.

"How would you like to join our team?" asked Iron Man.

It was everything Hawkeye could have wanted and more! He had been a young boy trying to find his place in the world, and now the best of the best wanted him to join their team. He was a real-life Super Hero!

Hawkeye felt like he could take on all the bad guys in the world, but his first mission with the Avengers was more than even he could have imagined.

"Grab your gear," Captain America said to the rest of the Avengers. "Ultron has reappeared with a robot army, and we're the only ones that can stop him!"

Ultron was a superintelligent robot. It was originally created to help the Avengers, but tragically, it went out of control! The Avengers were determined to capture the rogue robot.

Black Widow, Ant-Man and Wasp were able to track down Ultron to an abandoned car factory. Ultron had upgraded the facility. Now instead of making cars, it was making robotic copies of Ultron!

"You've fallen right into my trap," said Ultron, standing on a platform high above the ground. "Now my army of Ultrons will destroy you once and for all!"

Hawkeye shot his electric-net arrows at two of the robots, while Captain America, Black Widow, and the Hulk held off more fake Ultrons, making sure they couldn't attack. Ant-Man and the Wasp flew around disabling the machines, while Thor and Iron Man faced off against Ultron himself!

Ultron's robots were tough, but none of them could think for themselves, and the Avengers' powers were too much for the metallic foes.

Iron Man set his repulsor rays to full power and used them to stun Ultron!

"Well struck, Iron Man!" yelled Thor, excited to face off against evil, as always. "Now allow the son of Odin to finish the job!" Thor threw his mighty hammer, Mjölnir, forward at full speed, hitting Ultron and knocking him off his control platform.

"Show-off," muttered Iron Man. Their teamwork was too much for Ultron, who lay defeated.

The Mighty Avengers had saved the day!

"You know," Hawkeye said to Captain America, "when I got out of bed this morning, I wasn't expecting to fight an army of evil robots."

"Do you regret joining the Avengers?" asked Captain America.

"Are you kidding?" said Hawkeye with a smile. "We get to protect the world from evil! There's no place I'd rather be." Clint Barton knew that joining the Avengers was the best decision he ever made. And he couldn't wait to see what challenge they would face next!

Desert Brawl

Through his binoculars, General "Thunderbolt" Ross spotted a terrifying almost-seven-foot-tall creature causing havoc in the desert. Whatever it was, the beast was lifting up chunks of earth as if they were nothing! This creature could be very dangerous if he got close to the general's camp! The general knew the only thing that could stop this abomination was the Incredible Hulk. The general did not particularly like the Hulk, but he didn't have a choice. The general loudly ordered, "Send the Hulk out there!"

Once the Hulk arrived in the desert, he scanned his surroundings for the dangerous creature. It seemed like he was alone.

"Hulk doesn't see no one . . . puny general make mistake," the Hulk grunted.

Suddenly, a mighty fist hit the Hulk in the jaw! It was a surprise attack from the Abomination!

This made the Hulk mad. "Hulk think bad guy not playing fair!" the Hulk growled.

"No one can beat me! I am the Abomination!" The creature laughed.

But the Hulk quickly got back on his feet! With his fists in the air, he leaped high in the sky toward the Abomination. He wasn't going to give up without a good fight!

"Hulk smash!" the green goliath yelled. He knew he had to stop the Super Villain from hurting innocent people.

But the Abomination seemed just as strong as the Hulk!

"You dare to challenge me?" The Abomination smirked. "You know, even after my transformation, my mind still works perfectly—unlike your tiny brain!"

"Hulk think Abomination is fool to underestimate Hulk!" the hero yelled as he charged toward the Abomination. As the two large creatures collided, the whole desert shook!

When the Hulk finally shoved the Abomination off his
feet, the Hulk grabbed hold of the largest boulder he could
find. It must have weighed at least three tons, but the Hulk
lifted it high above his head with ease. The Incredible Hulk
was ready to stop the Abomination.

With all his might, the Hulk threw the boulder across the desert. The boulder skyrocketed up until no one could see it and then hurtled back down toward the Abomination. It looked like this might be the end for the evil creature.

To the Hulk's surprise, the Abomination instantly jumped back up without any problem. The Abomination clenched his hands into powerful fists and smashed the rock into a million pieces! The stone barely harmed him! It was as if Hulk just threw a snowball at him!

"Don't you know I'm just like you but *better*?" the Abomination said.

The Hulk shook his head. "Hulk think Abomination is just a bully! Hulk tired of hearing you talk!"

"Oh, you think you can handle the Abomination? I bet you can't!" the Abomination yelled, feeling more confident than ever that he could defeat the Hulk. This only made the Hulk angrier. The Hulk let out a loud roar from the pit of his stomach and, with all his energy, charged head-on into his enemy.

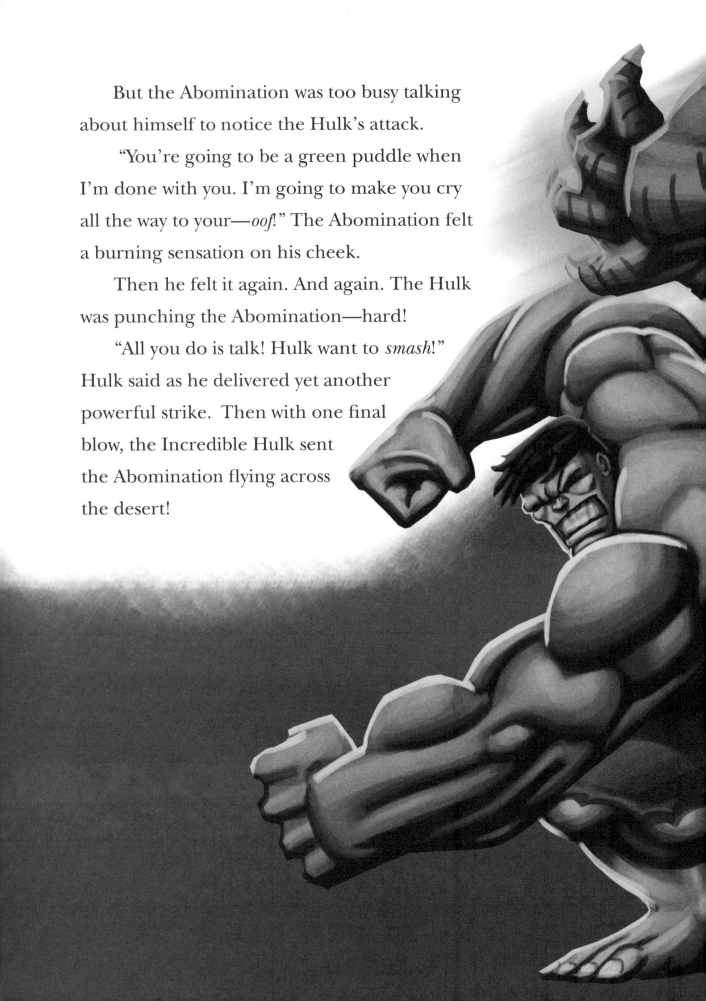

But the Abomination was too busy talking about himself to notice the Hulk's attack.

"You're going to be a green puddle when I'm done with you. I'm going to make you cry all the way to your—*oof!*" The Abomination felt a burning sensation on his cheek.

Then he felt it again. And again. The Hulk was punching the Abomination—hard!

"All you do is talk! Hulk want to *smash!*" Hulk said as he delivered yet another powerful strike. Then with one final blow, the Incredible Hulk sent the Abomination flying across the desert!

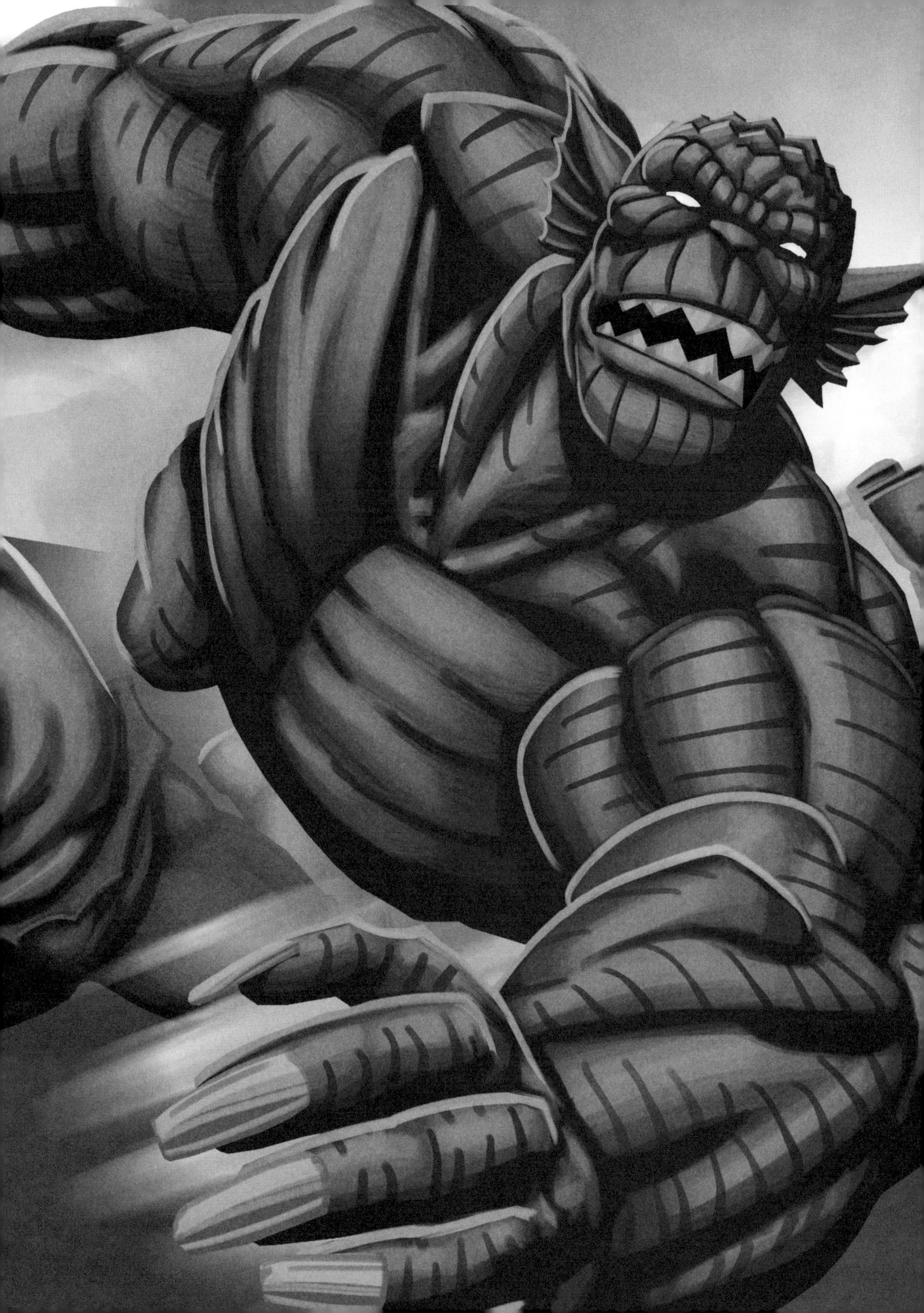

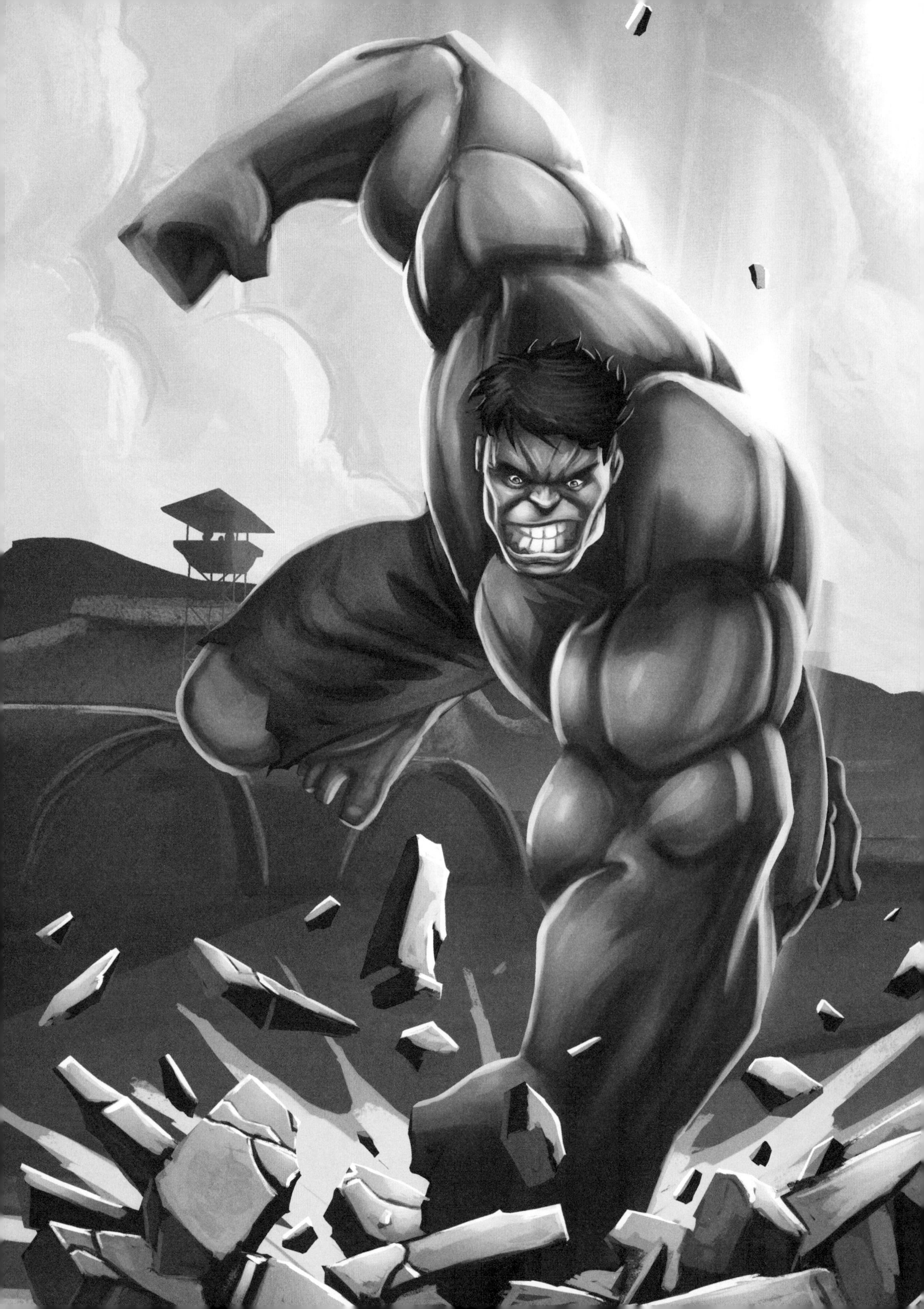

Watching closely, General Ross saw the Abomination go shooting across the desert and then burrow itself into the ground. It seemed like the creature would not be causing any more trouble. The Hulk defeated the Abomination!

Seconds later, there was a loud commotion outside. The general raced over to the scene. It was the Incredible Hulk! With a couple giant leaps, the Hulk had arrived in the middle of the general's camp. When he came down from the sky, he smashed his fist into the ground.

"What on earth are you doing?" the general shouted.

"Hulk just knocking to let you know he arrived."

"I don't think you had to do that. But you certainly did your job well fighting off the Abomination!" the general said.

"Yeah, you're a hero! You stopped him from hurting anyone," a soldier told the Hulk. There was a loud roar, and the Hulk turned his head to see all the soldiers cheering for the Incredible Hulk.

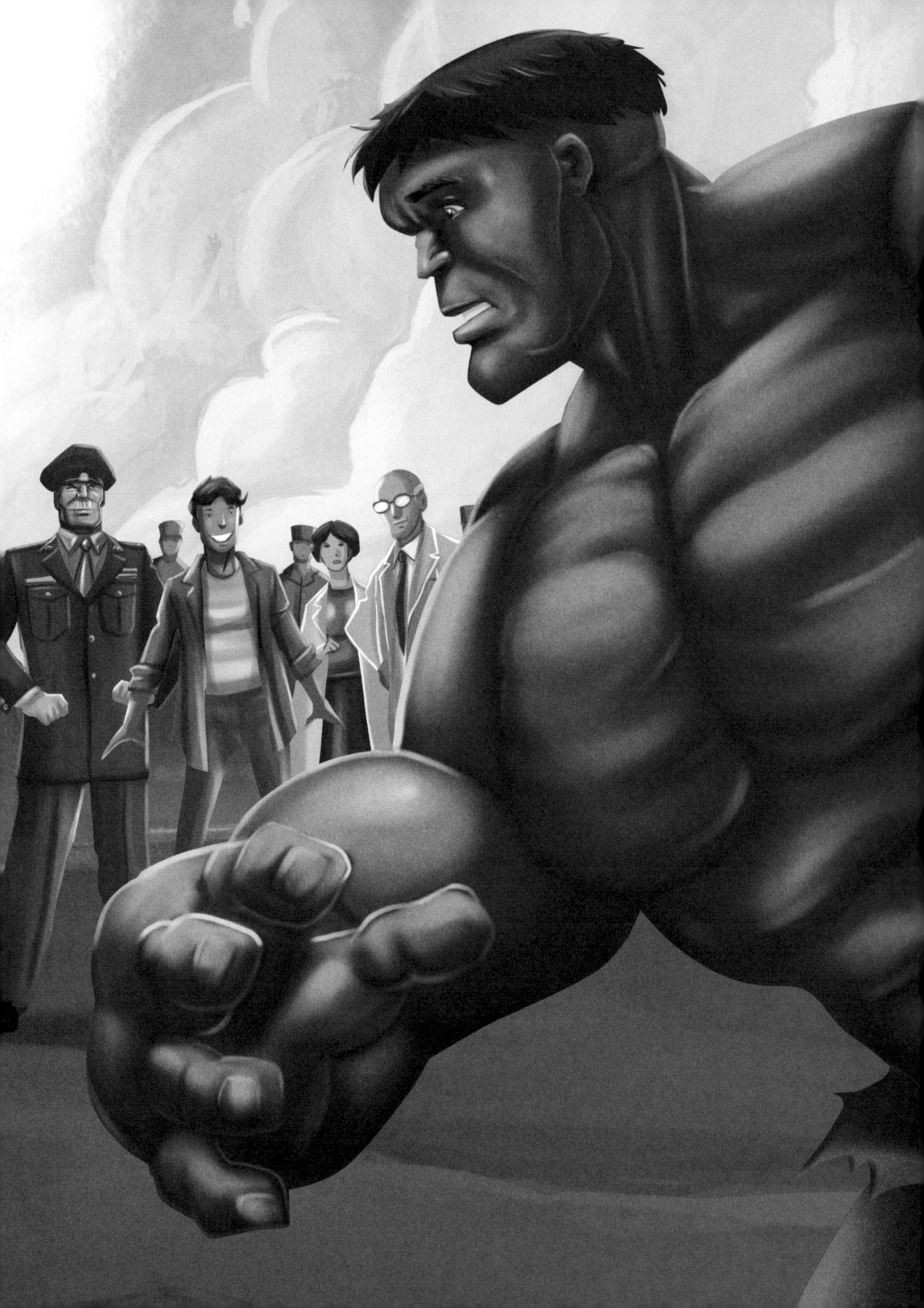

Suddenly, the Hulk felt strange. He wanted to get away from everyone. Within seconds, he leaped off into the desert. By the time he landed, he had changed back into Bruce Banner. No one had ever called the Hulk a hero before, Bruce thought. And for the first time, Bruce Banner believed the Hulk really could be an incredible hero.

Peter Parker's Pictures

Peter Parker loved his job as a photographer at *The Daily Bugle*, but sometimes his boss, J. Jonah Jameson, asked him to do the impossible.

"Parker, these photos you gave me for the last article aren't going to work!" he shouted as he ripped them apart. "If you want to keep taking pictures for *The Bugle*, you need to get exclusive shots. I'm about to run a feature on the Lizard. He's on the loose, and I need you to get me a close-up for the front page. Can you do it?"

"You can count on me, Mr. Jameson," Peter replied.

Truthfully, Peter Parker wasn't really thinking about the pictures—he was too focused on stopping the Lizard before he hurt anyone.

Peter knew that the Lizard was really Dr. Curtis Connors, a brilliant scientist who turned into the Lizard after a botched attempt at trying to grow back his missing arm. Now, like Peter, he had a secret identity. Dr. Connors wasn't a bad guy, but the Lizard was. Peter needed to transform him back to Dr. Connors. It was web-slinging time!

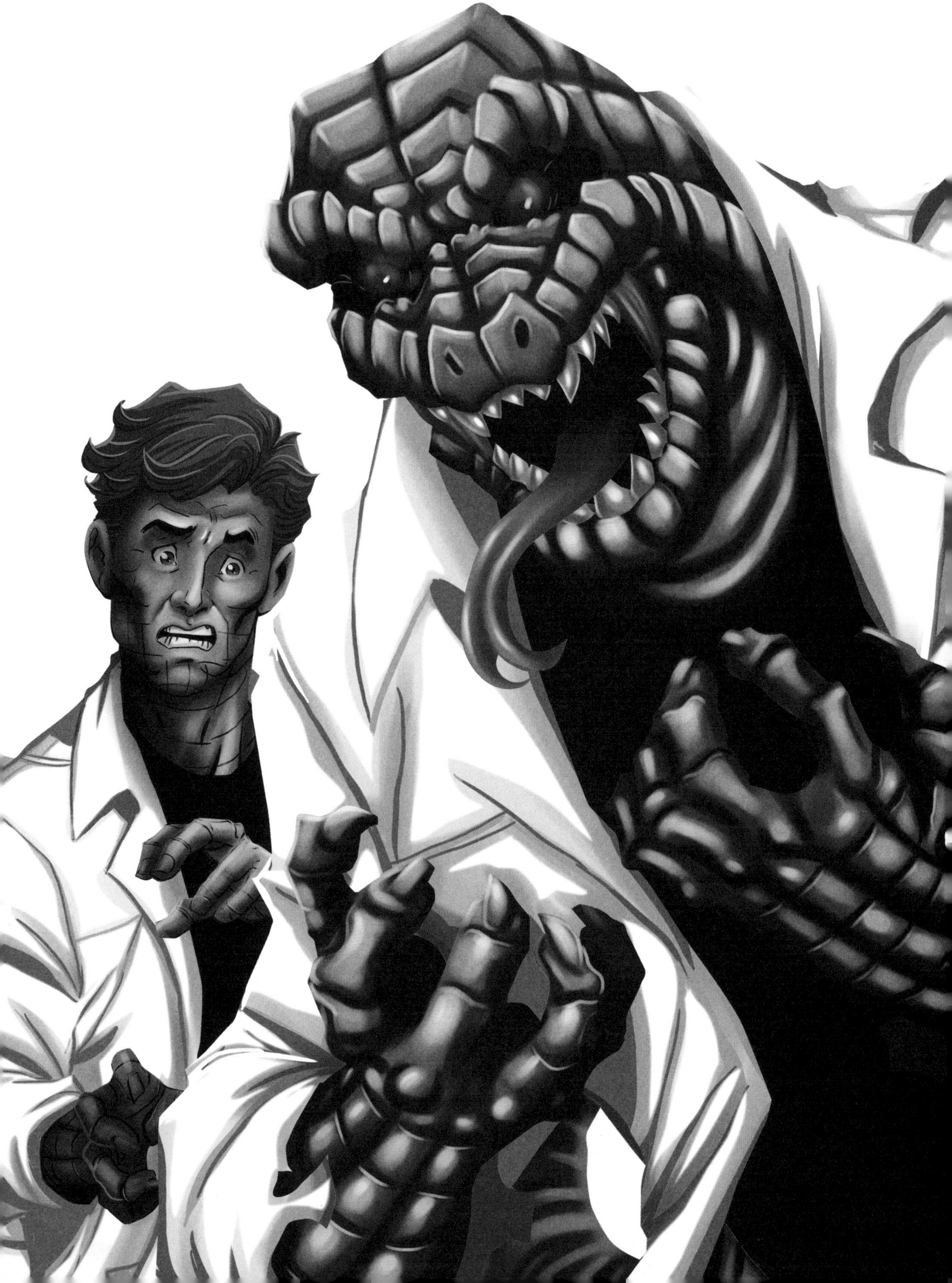

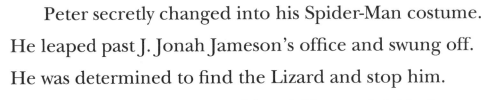

Peter secretly changed into his Spider-Man costume. He leaped past J. Jonah Jameson's office and swung off. He was determined to find the Lizard and stop him.

"I'm coming to get you, Lizard. You can't hide from the Amazing Spider-Man," Spidey said as he looked for the Lizard high above New York City.

Soon, Spider-Man spotted the Lizard crawling up the wall of a familiar building.

"Scaling the wall? And I thought you were a leapin' lizard," Spidey shouted as the Lizard tried to race ahead.

"You won't stop me!" the Lizard hissed as he jumped through a window and entered the building, which Spidey knew housed Dr. Connors's lab.

"Got you!" Spider-Man said as he found the Lizard inside the lab. Spidey shot a web at the Lizard, but the Lizard tore through it like it was paper. So much for catching him in a web, Spider-Man thought.

"I'm too strong for your weak web," the Lizard taunted.

Spider-Man raced toward the Lizard. "I have other tricks up my sleeve, Lizzy. Remember, there's no winning when you're a bad guy."

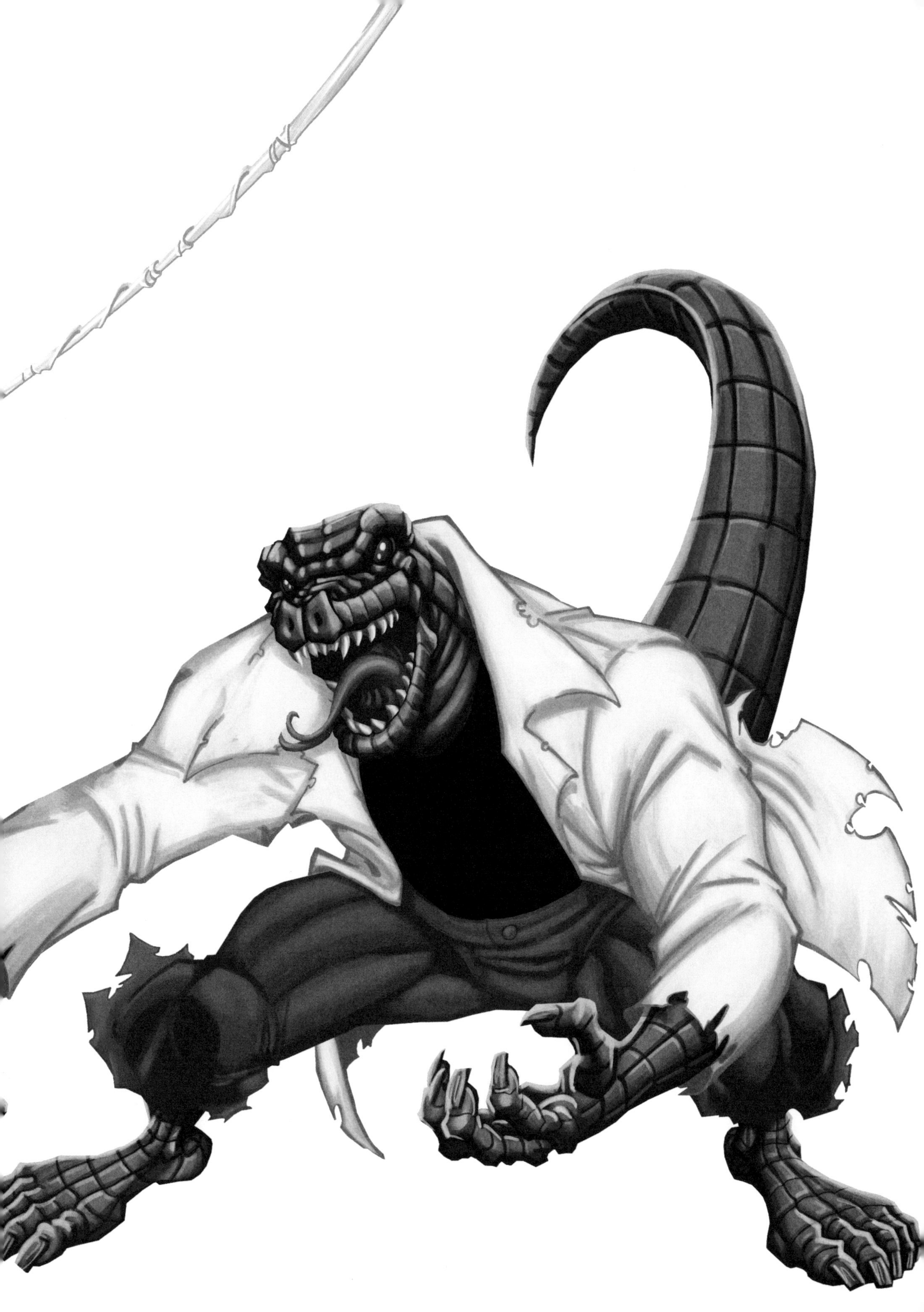

Spidey felt something bite his feet and realized that the Lizard had unleashed all the reptiles from the lab and had trained them to attack.

"Is this your version of a Lizard army? They won't stop the spectacular Spider-Man!" Spidey mocked the Lizard. Although he had to admit that the reptiles' bites were painful.

"I am going to make those reptiles grow bigger than I am. They will attack the city, and I shall rule them all," the Lizard said with an evil laugh.

"And you'll be the Lizard King?" Spider-Man questioned. "Not on my watch!"

Spider-Man shot a web and swung behind the Lizard, kicking him and knocking him to the ground. The monster was down, but not out.

The Lizard called to his army as he tried to get up. "Reptiles . . . attack!"

"Uh-oh," Spider-Man said. "I think I've just made him mad."

Just then, the Lizard leaped back up and started to attack Spider-Man again. Spidey worried that the Lizard and his army might be too much for him.

With all of his super spider-strength, Spider-Man delivered a powerful right cross to the Lizard, knocking him down with a thud!

Suddenly, the Lizard jumped back up and threw a desk at Spidey, who tripped over the sea of snakes and tiny lizards. Beneath his mask, Peter was worried he wouldn't win this battle and the Lizard might escape. He feared the villian would unleash the reptiles on the streets of New York and they would attack innocent people. Spidey had to act fast!

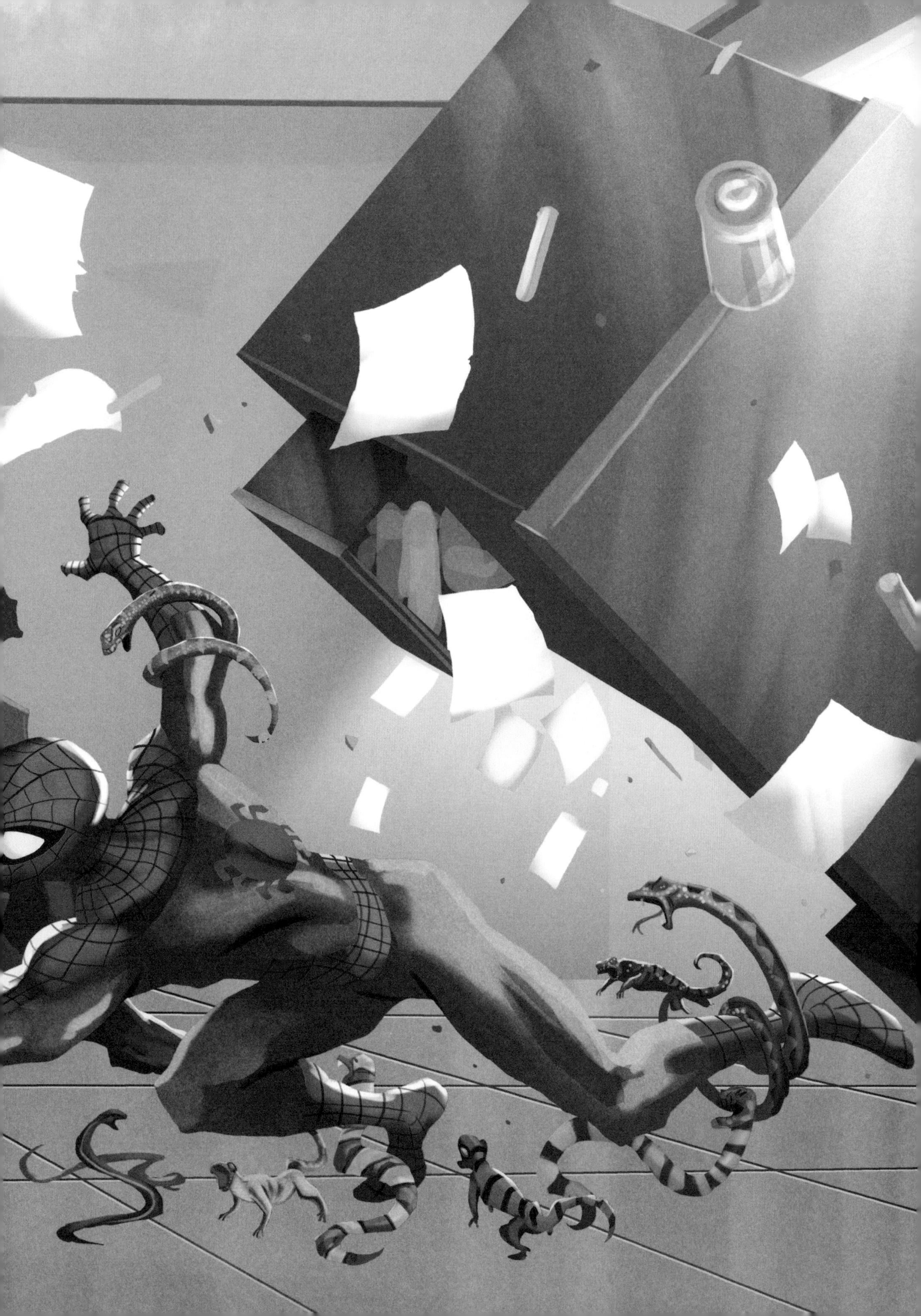

The Amazing Spider-Man jumped in front of the Lizard and
pushed him down with all his might! Then Spidey raced through
the lab to find a potion he knew would turn the Lizard back into
Dr. Connors.

When Spidey returned to the fight, the Lizard was enraged.
He was throwing lab equipment all around the room. He knew
he was trapped, and he didn't want Spider-Man to change him
back to Dr. Connors.

Even with snakes wrapped around his arms and legs, Spider-Man was able to pour the potion into the Lizard's mouth!

"Drink up, Lizzy. And let me welcome back Dr. Connors," Spider-Man said. He quickly remembered that he had to get a shot of the Lizard for *The Daily Bugle*. He took out his camera and snapped a picture of the Lizard before he transformed back into Dr. Connors.

"Spider-Man? What happened?" Dr. Connors asked as he looked around the lab, which was in shambles.

Spider-Man told Dr. Connors that he had once again transformed into the Lizard.

"I'm so glad to be back. Thank you, Spider-Man."

"And I'm glad to see you back to your old self, Doc," Spidey said. "The Lizard was attempting to train your reptiles to attack people. He wanted to make them enormous, so they could conquer all of New York."

"Oh, no," Dr. Connors said. He was very upset. "Luckily, you stopped him."

"Yes, and I think I'll take your formula with me for safe-keeping," Spider-Man said, holding up the potion that had cured Dr. Connors. Spider-Man wanted the potion at the ready in case he ever needed to rescue Dr. Connors again.

Later, Spider-Man was happy to be back at *The Daily Bugle* as Peter Parker.

J. Jonah Jameson yelled, "Parker! I need photos of the Lizard, and I need them now! Did you get them?"

Peter sat down and handed J. Jonah Jameson the photos.

"Now *these* are exclusive shots, Parker. Nice job. I don't know how a kid like you does it, but you always get close-ups. You have a talent. What's your secret?" J. Jonah Jameson asked.

Peter smiled. "Just lucky, I guess."

If only Jameson knew that Peter Parker was really the Amazing Spider-Man. Even if Peter told him, he probably wouldn't believe it. Some secrets are too hard to believe!

MARVEL
THE COURAGEOUS
CAPTAIN AMERICA™

The Lethal Lair of Red Skull

Private Steve Rogers was on leave in New York City. Normally, he was the hero Captain America, but right now Steve just wanted to be a citizen of the land he protected.

But Steve's rest and relaxation was interrupted when he got a call from General Phillips. "Captain America, we've uncovered Red Skull's newest evil plot!" Red Skull was an agent of HYDRA, a corrupt organization that would stop at nothing to prevent America from winning the World War.

"I'll be right there," Captain America said.

"Sorry solider, but we need you to sit this one out," the general said. "Intelligence says that Red Skull has found the plans for the Vita-Ray machine and now has a way to use it against you."

Captain America was shocked. He owed all his super strength to Vita-Rays. When combined with the Super-Soldier Serum, the Vita-Rays had changed the frail Steve Rogers into America's greatest protector, Captain America.

"Red Skull's calling it his 'Mortis-Ray.' If you were to be hit by its beam, you'd lose all your enhanced abilities," General Phillips said. "We can't risk you, son. The army is sending in a strike team as soon as they can spare the men. Stay away."

Captain America hung up the phone. He didn't want to disobey orders, but he couldn't let his fellow soldiers risk their lives for him. Could Cap break into Red Skull's base alone? It would be very dangerous.

As Cap looked around the streets of his beloved city, he knew what he had to do.

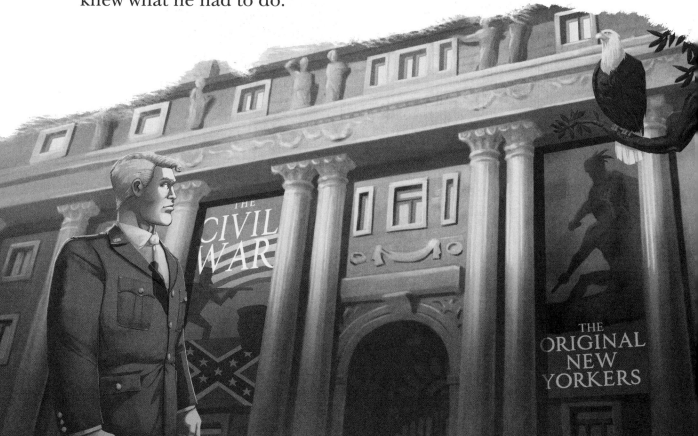

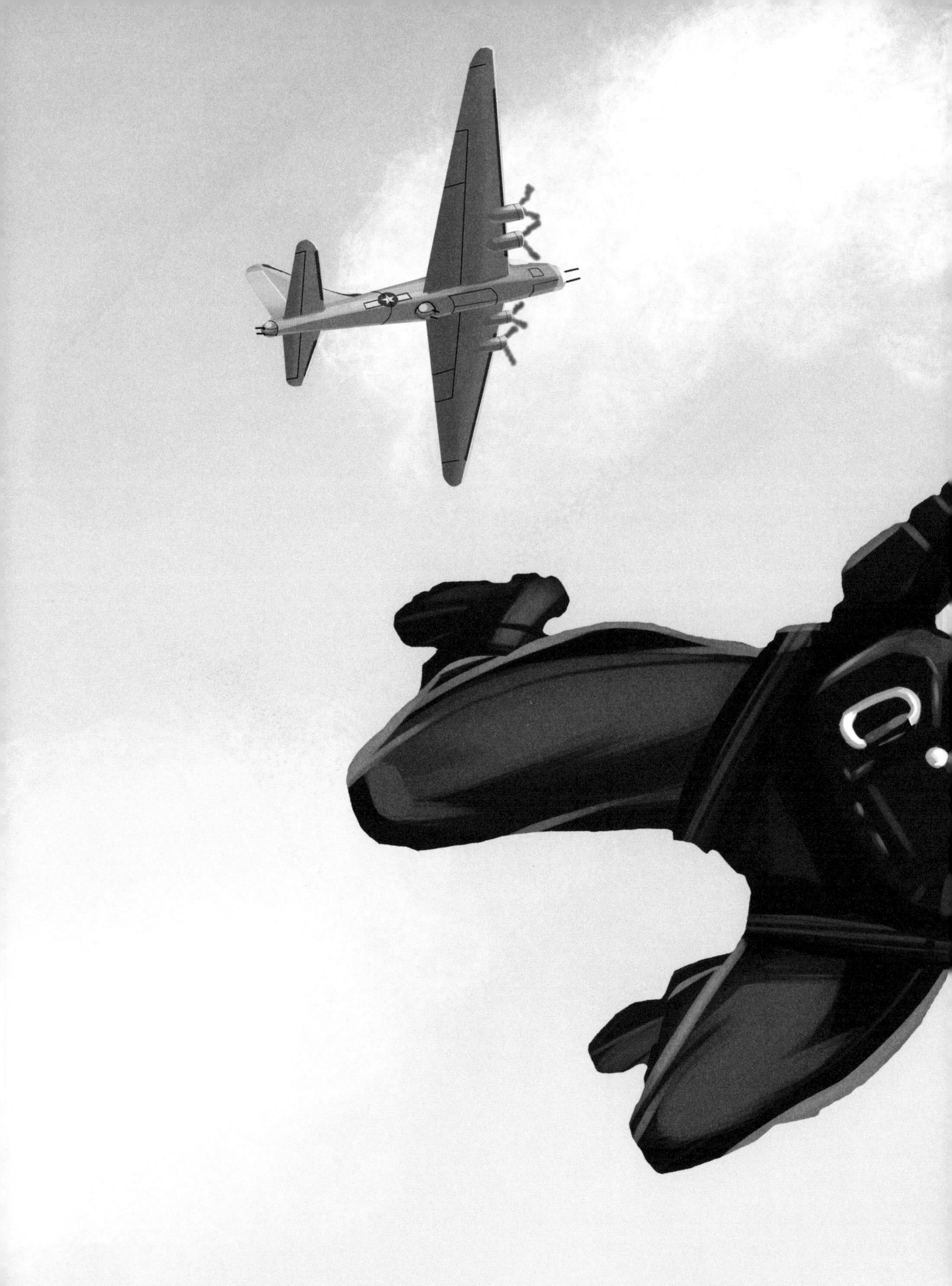

Twenty-four hours later, Captain America parachuted through the sky above Red Skull's lair.

HYDRA agents were everywhere as Cap slipped over the barbwire fence into enemy territory. There was no way he would be able to fight off all of them. Cap knew he would have to be stealthy to make it all the way to Red Skull's lab.

Suddenly, a guard turned the corner. Captain America didn't have enough time to hide.

"YOU!" The guard shouted. He was about to alert the entire base!

Without a moment's hesitation, Captain America raised his shield and prepared to fight. Before the guard could unholster his weapon, Cap knocked him to the ground with a strong right cross. The guard was out cold!

That was close, Captain America said to himself.

Cap quickly ran through the base, avoiding HYDRA patrols. Sometimes, however, the hero was forced to fight. But with the help of his vibranium shield and his quick wits, Captain America made his way closer and closer to the heart of Red Skull's lair. As Cap passed a winding stairway, he heard a familiar voice coming from below. It was Red Skull!

"Once we have robbed Captain America of his super strength, the world will be ours!"

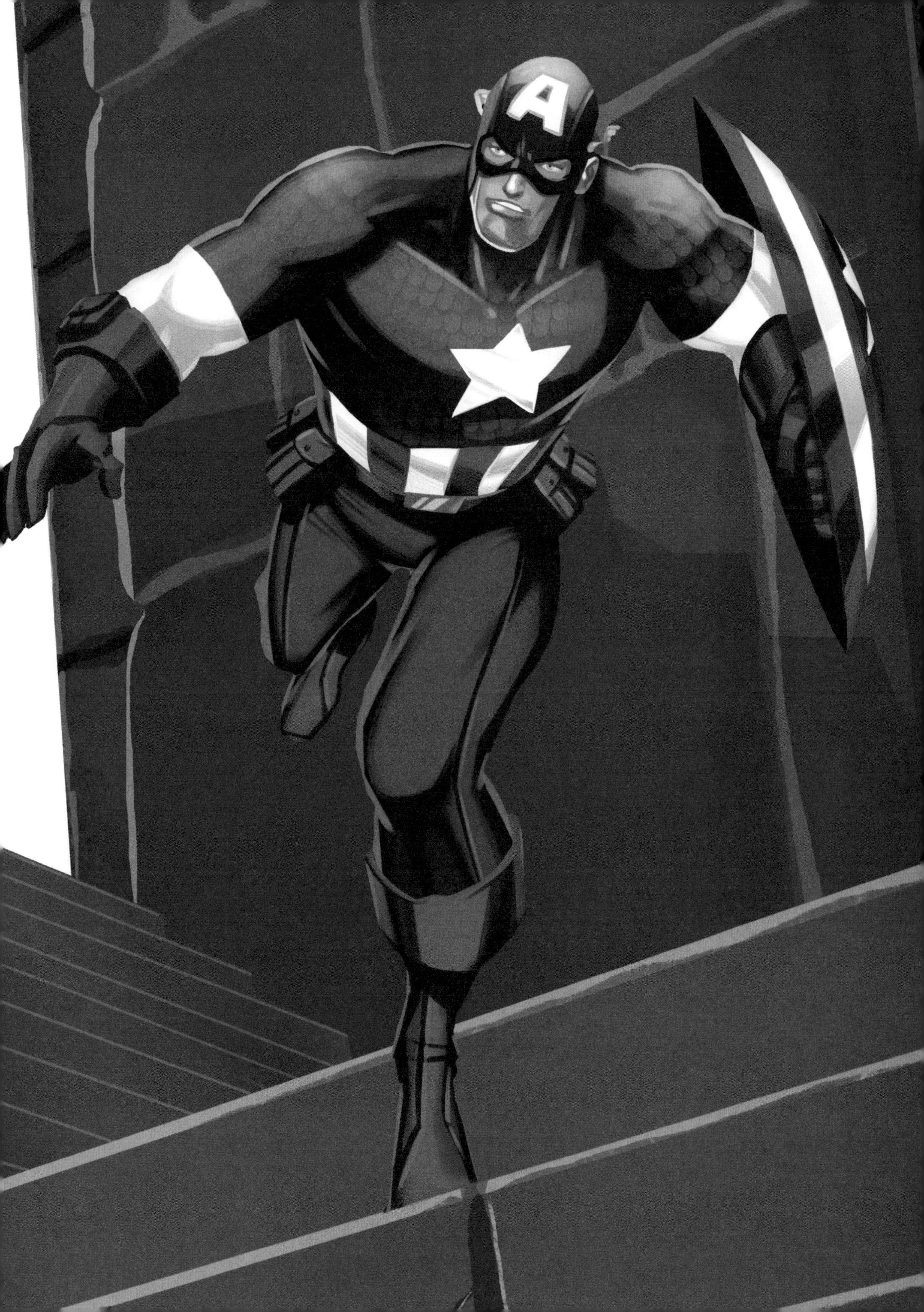

Cap knew that if he found Red Skull, the dastardly villain would lead him to the Mortis-Ray. Quietly, he crept down, following the raspy voice of the HYDRA agent. Red Skull's secret lab had to be close by. Suddenly, Captain America turned a corner—and was face-to-face with Red Skull. America's great protector had found Red Skull, but Red Skull had also found him!

"Welcome to my lab, Captain America," Red Skull said. "You heroic fool. You've saved me the trouble of hunting you down." He stepped menacingly toward Cap. "Once I use my Mortis-Ray and remove your super strength, there will be no one to defend your precious America!"

"I won't let you win, Red Skull!" Captain America shouted. With a great leap, Captain America kicked Red Skull, sending him hurtling toward the ground. But to Captain America's surprise, Red Skull just laughed.

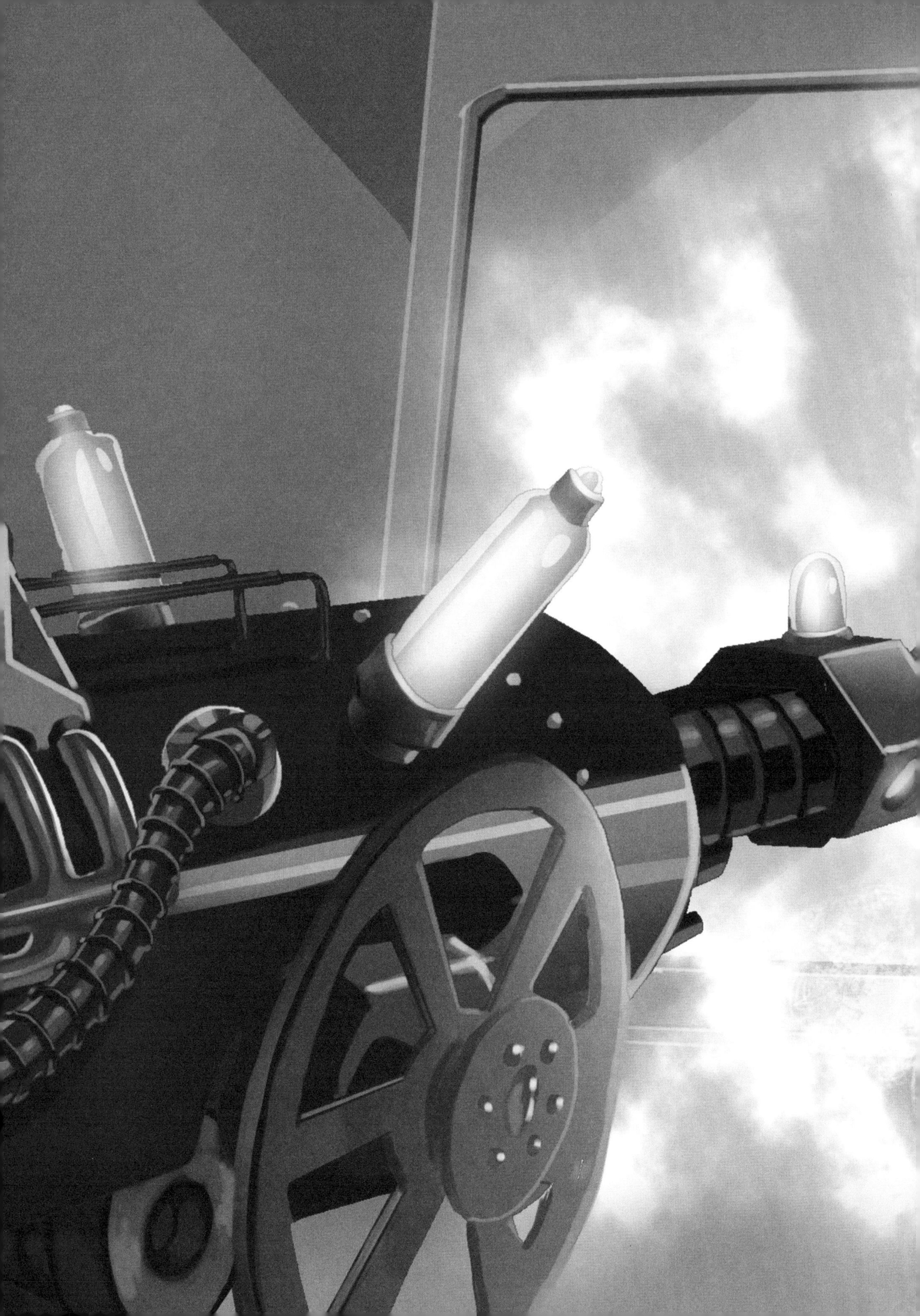

"You think that you could defeat me with a simple kick?" Red Skull taunted as he held up a remote conrol device. Looking up, the hero realized that Red Skull had led him right into the path of the Mortis-Ray!

With a final, mirthless laugh, Red Skull hit the switch and the machine activated. Captain America was caught in its beam!

Captain America's legs began to weaken. Suddenly his shield felt heavy on his arm. Cap knew if he didn't do something soon, he would be the frail Steve Rogers again, powerless to stop Red Skull. With the last of his strength, Captain America raised his shield and hurled it at the Mortis-Ray machine. Red Skull screamed in horror as the powerful shield hit the machine.

As the Mortis-Ray sputtered and sparked, Captain America realized it was about to explode! Quickly, Cap pulled his shield from the twisted metal and leaped away. The device detonated with a fiery blast, destroying Red Skull's lethal lab.

But as Cap looked back at the wreckage, he didn't see Red Skull anywhere. He must have escaped during the explosion! Cap thought. Red Skull would have to meet justice another day.

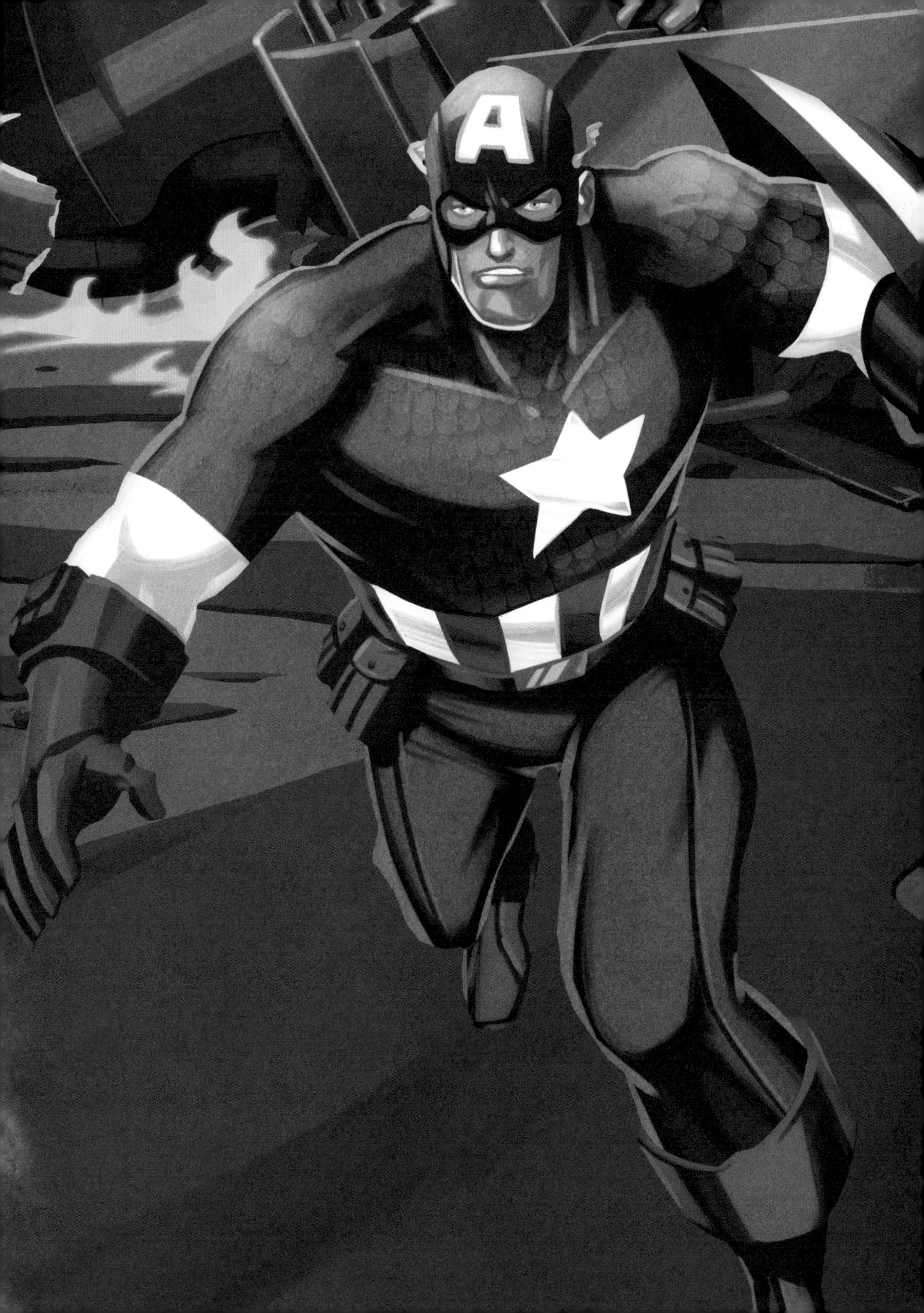

As Cap made his way out of the ruined lab, he thought about what he would tell General Phillips. Cap had disobeyed orders, but he had done it to save others. He hoped that the general would understand.

Cap flexed his arm, smiling down at his trusty shield. He was thankful that the Mortis-Ray's effects had only been temporary. Captain America still had his powers, and America still had its great protector.